Book One:

Courage, Love, and the

Meaning of

Christmas

A Christmas Adventure-Romance Novel

Book Two: The Perfect Gift
Book Three: The Art of Heart

by Shaun Roundy

2nd Edition
© 2023 The University of Life Press
UofLIFE.com/books
ISBN 978-1-893594-29-6

READER COMMENTS

"Roundy is a pro in this genre. He really captures the heart of interpersonal interactions and relationships, and mixes in the right amount of suspense and adventure. And he takes a much needed and profound look at the real meaning and purpose of life. An excellent read!"

"I really loved this book. I read it in two nights -- practically couldn't put it down."

"The story is interesting and moving, the writing is vivid, the characters are well defined, I learned a lot about the meaning of life, but mostly, it was really fun to read. I rarely read the same thing twice, but this once I certainly will."

"I laughed. I cried. The story stuck with me and made me think...about the meaning of life. ...The characters wriggled their way into my heart."

"From the start it gave me a new way to think about life."

"I took it with me on vacation to Kauai and read it on the airplane instead of looking out the window at the beautiful tvolcanic islands below me. I read it laying on the beach instead of going for an early morning snorkel. I read it in the car instead of admiring all the beautiful scenery on the Garden Island, but I don't feel like I missed out on anything."

"It's easy reading but thought provoking and inspiring."

"It was so easy to imagine myself as the character in the story, to feel like I was the one having the adventure."

"I could not put it down and when I got to the end, I wanted to start over so that I would not have to quit reading/living the adventure."

"This is seriously one of the best books that I've read."

DEDICATED TO THE MEMORY OF
SPENCER SMITH
1975-1996

"I recommend this series of books to anyone who loves to read. Shawn knows how to keep your interest to the point that you can not put the book down. It's very rare that I find a book like that and this series does that!!!"

"I gave it out to a couple of people for Christmas presents, and they have come back to buy more and give them to their friends. I highly, highly recommend this book."

"Totally believable adventure romance."

"Finally no sex, no drugs, no illicit affairs. This is a book to think about. You will contemplate along with the characters and stretch your thoughts along the way. Excellent book!"

"Shaun has a style that puts the reader right in the situation, as if you were actually there."

"Down to earth, soul searching, inspiring!!!"

"It is certainly a keeper, a re-reader."

"I laughed. I cried. The story stuck with me and made me think. I, like Spencer, thought about the meaning of life. As I read this thoughts and the characters wriggled their way into my heart. After I finished, I found these thoughts had blossomed and I will be better for having read this."

1 Dreams Come True

The white vapor of my breath hung in the cold air as I locked the car door and turned to Julie, already standing in her cross-country skis on the snow-covered road and waiting for me impatiently.

"Hurry up, slowpoke," she said with a happy grin, her pretty blonde hair brushing the shoulders of a sky-blue parka.

I smiled back and stepped toward her while sliding my wrists through the pole straps, then pressed the toes of my boots into my ski bindings until they clicked into place. All my fondest dreams were coming true.

Daylight drained slowly from the pale Christmas Eve sky toward the distant western horizon, while thick, heavy clouds packed cozily against the mountainside above us like a giant down comforter.

"Let's go!" I said, nodding toward the canyon, and we began sliding up the snowy road, pushing ourselves forward with our long poles, stepping forward and gliding several inches with each step.

Warm city lights reflected from the clouds' bellies and lit the way before us. As I glanced up, a tiny crystal snowflake landed on my nose and melted instantly.

Tonight's first date with my dream girl began earlier this afternoon when I bumped into Julie on campus. "Hi, Spencer," she said with a smile as we passed each other on the sidewalk.

"Hi, Julie," I replied.

Courage, Love and the Meaning of Christmas

Then we both stopped in our tracks and turned to each other with a look of pleasant surprise on our faces. "How do you know my name?" we both said at once, then laughed together and neither of us answered the question.

Despite taking a philosophy class together all semester long, we had never actually met. Not because I didn't want to. Not because I wasn't interested. Her pretty face and intelligent, happy, bright-blue eyes caught my attention from day one and I had watched her ever since, enduring a pleasant crush only from a distance thanks to my shyness.

But once we started talking, everything fell right into place. She asked lots of questions about me and I answered and tried to find out more about her, but she seemed more interested in me than telling about herself. We eventually wandered over to the Student Center for a cup of hot chocolate, and then I suggested cross-country skiing. Her eyes lit up with excitement, and twenty minutes later we found ourselves here, with an entire canyon, an entire mountain, an entire world all to ourselves.

All my fondest dreams were coming true.

Snow began falling harder as we skied deeper into the mountains, its crystal flakes making a quiet tinkling sound against our parkas as we slid forward first on one ski, then the other, pushing with our poles and gliding along the trail as it climbed slowly upward.

After several miles, the trail flattened out and we slid to a stop, side by side, in a tiny clearing, and caught our breath. Tall pines and bare aspen trunks hemmed in the snowy meadow, while just enough light reflected down from the clouds to illuminate the scene.

"It's so beautiful," Julie whispered under her breath.

I turned to her and nodded. "I knew you'd like it."

I clicked out of my ski bindings and my boots sank five inches into the snow when I stepped over Julie's skis to face her. She now stood eye to eye with me - and mouth to mouth, I couldn't help but notice. Even in the growing darkness of the approaching night, her bright blue eyes sparkled happily.

A snowflake landed on her warm cheek and melted instantly, leaving a tiny drop of cool water than slid down her cheek to her chin. I reached out a gloved hand and wiped the drop away.

Julie looked down shyly for a moment as I stepped even closer, then she raised her chin defiantly, refusing to display the excitement and intimidation she was feeling.

I slipped the pack from my shoulders and dropped it in the snow to one side, then took another step closer to Julie, our faces now only a few inches apart. Her confidence waivered visibly as I drew even closer, and she struggled to hide the fact that her heart was beating quickly, pounding hard behind her ribs.

One corner of her mouth turned up in a faint smile as I reached one arm around her waist, and then she threw both arms around my neck and pulled her slender body tightly against mine.

We stood that way without speaking for over a minute, and when I finally began to let go and back away, she glanced momentarily into my eyes, then pulled me forward again, face to face, mouth to mouth, her warm, pink lips pressed softly against mine. She ran her gloved hand through my hair, then squeezed me even tighter with her other arm, pausing only long enough to whisper "Oh, Spencer, I...I think I love you!"

All my fondest dreams were coming true.

2 Truth and Freedom

Fondest *day* dreams, that is.

My mind snapped back from my imaginary ski date to philosophy 1010. Julie sat at her desk across the room, utterly unaware of my existence. All semester long I had wanted to get to know her and wished for the courage to do something about it – walk up and say hi, ask to borrow a pen, ask her out, anything – but fear of failure – certain, absolute, guaranteed, humiliating failure – had prevented me from trying.

So here I sat, with my roommate and best friend, enjoying my futile crush from across the room.

Meanwhile, the professor droned on about "the problem of human freedom." Apparently certain philosophers couldn't reconcile God's omniscience with the idea that we humans have any ability to choose for ourselves. Apparently if God knows the future, then we are powerless to change it. Apparently, everything that ever happens was destined by God's foreknowledge.

Duh! I thought for the umpteenth time. I didn't understand how all those philosophers could be so dense. *Knowing* isn't a causal factor. I know that the sun will rise tomorrow, for example, but my knowing doesn't make it so. My knowing is secondary to the fact. If the sun decided, on a whim, to take the day off, I would be powerless to stop it.

Courage, Love and the Meaning of Christmas

Divine omniscience and human freedom are two separate things. If I decided to take a different route home from class, or suddenly change my major, or even change my personality and the entire course of my life, it would be because I chose to change, and worked at it, or learned something that made it possible. No amount of God saying, "I knew it! I knew you were going to do that!" would make Him entirely responsible for my decisions.

Of course, He could cause things to happen which would influence my future, but even then it would be His actions, not his foreknowledge, that caused the effect. And even then, to whatever degree I was able to make choices, I would be the one responsible for the change.

I felt bored of philosophy. What had induced me to consider changing my major to it? I guess it was my best friend Ski, who I first met in this class and who now sat to my right. The philosophical questions he often posed seemed much more interesting than the ones we debated endlessly in class. They seemed important, applicable to life, and I always wanted to get to the bottom of our challenging discussions. He had a way of turning his deep questions into contests and games, which made them even more fun.

My roommate Ben sat to my left. Brilliant but boring. Simultaneously superior and insecure. He had a way of turning the contest of wits into a contest of egos. Other than that, he was a nice enough guy.

Or maybe it was Julie. She always made class more interesting, but that had nothing to do with philosophy itself. I had stolen glances at her all semester long, but we had never spoken a word.

Unlike my daydreams, and unlike my conversations with Ski, I didn't have the confidence to talk to her. What would I say? What would she say? What would I say then?

Once or twice I tried to speak up as we shuffled out of class, but the words froze in my throat, paralyzed by the certainty that even if I managed to sound suave At first,, I'd quickly blow my cover and reveal what a shy, awkward, uninteresting boy I was.

I had to thank my shyness for saving me from that kind of embarrassment. Thanks to my inability to talk to Julie, I could at least enjoy daydreaming about her with no humiliating memories to interfere.

As the professor reviewed details about the final exam in a few days, I watched Julie's blonde hair tumble across her shoulders as she whispered to her friends. Today was the last class of the semester. The last chance to talk to Julie while we still had something in common.

I glanced at my notes and saw the last thing I had written: "The problem of human freedom." Yes, I was free to try to talk to Julie - that much lay within my power. But I would just crash and burn. I was not free to make a good impression, make her laugh, or persuade her to go out with me.

The problem with human freedom, I thought to myself, is that we can choose our actions, but we can't choose the results.

Class ended and everyone picked up their backpacks and headed for the door. Time was running out. I thought of getting to the end of my row of seats in time to say hi to Julie as she walked past, but she was surrounded by her friends, as always, and I knew I wouldn't try.

Ski glanced back and forth between Julie and I, then abruptly stood and left the room.

"Where's he going in such a hurry?" asked Ben.

3 Audacious

"I'm bored," Ski announced decidedly, reaching across the table and shutting the biology textbook I was trying to digest. We had come to the library to cram for what promised to be a long night. "Let's get out of here."

"I can't," I said. "Gotta study." I began to open my text to search for my place but Ski slapped it shut again.

"Let's do something," he insisted. "You'll study better after taking a break."

"There's no time for a break. My final's at seven a.m. I have to finish three more chapters tonight and review six pages of notes. It's comprehensive."

"It'll just take a minute," Ski assured me. "We'll chuck some snowballs at cars or get a snack and then come right back and you'll be amazed at how much smarter you became."

"Go away, please," I said, sliding my book down the table away from him and opening the cover again. "Not everyone can be a genius like you."

It was true. Ski was book smart. He read quickly and retained enough details to get straight A's without much effort.

"Spencer," Ski began again, "I'm asking you this favor as a friend. It's important. I'm bored."

Ski was clever as well. He had a way of twisting everything to his advantage. I usually enjoyed the challenge of keeping up with his subtle and not-so-subtle manipulations, but not tonight. I shook my head, found my place, and began to read.

"Frankly, Spencer, I'm shocked that you value our friendship so lightly. After all I've done for you...."

"*To* me," I corrected. Ski was also extremely sarcastic and the biggest practical joker I had ever met, though his sense of humor was more subtle than most.

"What about all the women I've introduced you to?"

"Shhh. I'm trying to read."

"What about Janie?" Ski interrupted again. "She was beautiful, she was intelligent, she was charming...."

"You told her I was a reporter from TMZ working undercover to secretly interview beautiful coeds and shoot an exposé on the country's ten hottest campuses."

"Well I had to tell her *something* to convince her to go out with you."

"Then you told her I was dying of cancer."

"I had to tell her *something* to explain your shyness and why sometimes you didn't have anything to say because...."

"...Because life is so precious and I didn't know how I would ever let it go."

Ski paused for a moment. "I admit, that was not my finest moment." He thought for a moment longer, then began again. "What about Carissa? She was...."

My expression stopped him. Carissa was fascinating and fun and came into my life periodically, just long enough to win my trust and make me addicted to her again before vanishing for weeks at a time when she wouldn't drop by or answer my calls, long enough to spoil most of the good memories.

"I see your point," Ski conceded.

Despite any trouble Ski had caused me over the few months we had known each other, I had to admit that I enjoyed his friendship and admired his audacity, which happened to be my greatest weakness.

I wasn't a coward, exactly, but I could be shy and rarely tried to change. What for? Whenever I tried, I only made things worse. I looked like an idiot and my fear of fear itself only increased. If I kept my mouth closed and let Ski do most of the talking, then I could at least appear audacious by association. It felt good. It felt exciting. It inspired me to at least dream about overcoming my shyness someday. Maybe if I dreamt about it long enough, that would count as practicing, and I'd eventually be able to do it for real.

As Ski worked on his next argument, the door to the study room opened and a brunette walked in and made her way to the far end of the long oak table.

"Hi," Ski offered as she walked by.

"Hi," she answered without taking much notice of either of us. She opened her backpack and pulled a few heavy political science textbooks from inside. Ski watched her for a moment while he formulated his plan.

"Excuse me," he interrupted, "can I ask your opinion on something?" The girl looked up but didn't speak. "What's your name?"

"Lauren," she answered expressionlessly. She looked like the conversation had already taken up too much precious time.

"Lauren, my friend Spencer here has one more year left before graduating in pre-law. He has a shot at valedictorian and the Presidential Fellowship. But his parents say if he doesn't have a girlfriend by the time he goes home for Christmas, they want him to stay home and take over the family business. He broke up with a girlfriend at the beginning of the semester and says he can't find anyone to date who's interested enough in her studies."

Lauren's face had become a mixture of incredulity and annoyance, but at least Ski had captured her attention.

"Now, I'm not asking you to be his girlfriend, even though he is very intelligent and charming, but would you be willing to make an appearance with him at lunch tomorrow when his parents drop in?"

Lauren looked at me and back at Ski, one eyebrow raising while the opposite corner of her mouth rose in a slight sneer.

"His parents run a political think tank back east, so they want him to take care of the sailboat sales shop in Virginia Beach."

Lauren let out a little sigh, but her expression gave no clue about her reaction.

"Tell you what," Ski tried again, "just join us for a quick bite tonight and you can decide if it's worth your time. That way, if it works out, you'll at least be acquainted."

"Sorry," Lauren finally said. "Gotta study."

"Listen," Ski began, changing strategies, "the truth is that Spencer saw you at the student center and has had a crush on you all semester but didn't have the courage to ask you out. Sorry about the whole story

Courage, Love and the Meaning of Christmas

thing," he added with an apologetic shrug.

"If it wasn't finals," Lauren said with a very slight smile, "you *might* be funny." With that, she piled her books back into her pack, slung it over one shoulder, and left the room.

After a minute of quiet and just as I began to read again, Ski broke the silence. "I *can't believe* you let her get away," he said, shaking his head. "She's smart. She's a keeper."

4 The Meaning of Life

I sat in the computer lab the following afternoon and stared at the monitor. My biology final hadn't gone as well as I hoped, but I felt relieved to have it over just the same. Now I could focus on my remaining two finals and the philosophy paper sitting motionless on the computer screen.

I had filled the required ten pages with ideas and quotes, but couldn't come up with any kind of conclusion. This didn't surprise me since I had no idea what anybody was supposed to learn from my paper.

The paper was titled "The Meaning of Life." I began the semester optimistically, and in my foolish enthusiasm, determined to discover and reveal the meaning of life in ten short pages. My professor had tried to dissuade me, but I would not give up. "I have the entire semester," I reasoned, "it can't be that hard."

I was wrong. I skimmed the musings of ancient and modern philosophers, psychologists, religious leaders, even musicians, and found a few good insights, but nothing capable of definitively defining what 'the meaning of life' means nor discovering the secret of how to achieve a meaningful life.

I did succeed in finding plenty of contradiction, however.

Kant, for example, considers only the intention behind actions in determining the value of one course of action or another. The "right" choice may result in suffering rather than success and satisfaction.

Such principle-based living may provide direction, and doing what's right will surely bring about some satisfaction, but there's no guarantee it will lead to a truly meaningful life.

Mills' practical utilitarianism, on the other hand, looks at the ends rather than the means. Whatever brings the greatest happiness to the greatest number of people, he taught, is the correct course of action.

If everyone adopted and applied this philosophy faithfully, then perhaps everyone would find life meaningful and happy. Countless experiments, however, demonstrate that humans tend to act selfishly and from a fear of scarcity. No modern utopian experiment has ever succeeded and endured.

Sartre, Becket and other existentialists suggest that life is inherently arbitrary. Meaning – if such a thing exists – is fleeting and insignificant.

Modern philosophers of language engage in arcane discussions about the shades of meaning of the word 'meaning', but I could never extract any useful ideas from their expositions.

Studying other fields didn't help much, either. Freud had a major impact on the development of modern psychology, but his oversimplified assertion that we're driven toward pleasure and away from pain seemed to describe only the animal side of humankind and doesn't serve as a very detailed nor effective guide to creating a satisfying, meaningful life, because even continual pleasure can not create an unlimited supply of meaning.

A hundred years of psychology had focused almost exclusively on what's *wrong* with people rather than what's right. I didn't expect to learn much about meaning by studying emotional trauma, schizophrenia and phobias.

Christianity advises losing oneself in service to others. "He who loses his life shall find it," Jesus teaches, but comprehension of such doctrine requires first-hand experience, not merely rhetoric, so my paper could not convincingly explain that solution.

The Beatles sing that "all you need is love," but just because you wanna hold someone's hand doesn't mean the feeling will be reciprocated, or that it will endure and result in a meaningful life.

Reading my paper almost had the effect of leaving readers more confused about the meaning of life than they began. I frequently considered changing the title to "The Meaninglessness of Life."

Someone walked behind me and kicked my chair on the way past. "Hey, Spence," Adam said, sitting down at the next computer. "Almost done?"

"Hey Adam," I replied. "Sort of."

"How can you be sort of almost done?" he asked, unzipping his backpack and peering inside. "You either are or you aren't."

"I'm almost done," I explained, "but I'm stuck on the conclusion."

"Got it," Adam replied, and began rummaging through his pack for his flash drive. When he didn't find it, he began emptying the pack's contents onto the table, pulling out handfuls of sunscreen tubes, chemical hand warmers, and energy bars. Adam worked at the Outdoor Recreation Center on campus and spent most of his time outdoors, making the most of the local mountains and his free equipment rentals. His bright-green eyes glowed with energy and showed none of the stress and fatigue evident in most students' expressions in the room. His tan face and muscular arms boasted of a summer spent scaling mountain crags and an early winter chasing first tracks on back-country telemark skis. He finally located the tiny flash drive and plugged it into the computer's USB port.

"What about you?" I asked. "Almost done?"

"Far from it, bro," he answered, grinning proudly about his slacker ways.

"Have you even started your paper?"

"Sort of," Adam answered evasively.

"How can you have 'sort of' started?" I asked. "You either have or you haven't."

"I brainstormed up some killer topic ideas on the way over," he explained.

I shook my head in mock disappointment. "You'll pay dearly for your procrastination, young man."

"A small price to pay for another semester full of fresh air, first tracks and freedom." Adam took a deep, satisfying breath and his eyes got a distant look in them. "Seriously, man," he added, focusing on me again, "you look drained. You work way too hard."

"Yeah, maybe so," I admitted. "Anyway, I've had all I can take for right now." I hit the print button for my paper, then closed the document and packed up my papers and books to leave. "See you at the study session tomorrow night?" I asked.

"Can't," Adam said without looking up. "Got a hot date." He glanced over then and raised one eyebrow momentarily like a reverse wink. "You gonna get me some answers to the study guide?"

"Maybe. You gonna line me up with one of your ex-girlfriends?"

"Whatever," Adam answered, waving one hand dismissively through the air. "You've got plenty of girls!" Adam had no idea what a big liar Ski was and believed every story he weaved about my various fictional romantic exploits.

"A small price to pay for a semester's worth of studying," I pointed out.

"Yeah, yeah, whatever," he shrugged me off.

"Hey, you don't happen to know the meaning of life, do you?" I asked as I stood up to leave. Who knows? Maybe all that time spent far away from the hustle and bustle of modern life and out in the peaceful mountains had led him to some great epiphany that could complete my paper.

"Of course," he answered confidently, raising an eyebrow again as if shocked that I would ask such an obvious question. I raised an inquisitive eyebrow back at him, wondering if I succeeded at looking skeptical. "Play hard," Adam began, "then play even harder."

"Seems to work for *you*," I conceded.

"Try it sometime," he insisted, "and you'll discover that everything you need falls right into your lap."

"Yeah, yeah," I replied. "Whatever."

"Later, man."

Half a dozen students crowded around the lab assistant's desk waiting for either a free computer or their print outs. "Meaning of life?" the assistant asked, and handed me my paper when I raised my hand. I pounded a staple into the corner and turned around while shoving the paper into my pack.

As I turned, I bumped into someone who had stepped up behind me. "Sorry 'bout that," I said as I looked up into Julie's bright-blue eyes.

"That's alright," she smiled back, then began stepping around me to sign up on the waiting list.

"Hey, Julie," I said before I could stop myself. Her expression told me that she was surprised to hear her name and was struggling to remember where she had seen me before. "Are you working on your philosophy paper?" I knew it was a stupid question to ask someone I'd never spoken to before, but our surprise meeting hadn't given me enough time to get nervous and my voice sounded calm and confident.

"Uh, huh," she answered, finally placing my face.

"Gonna make the deadline?" I asked.

"I think so," she affirmed.

"Well good luck with that," I said, eager to end the conversation before I got nervous and our conversation grew truly awkward. "I won't keep you."

"Okay," she nodded agreeably. "Bye."

I nodded to her with my last ounce of false confidence, then turned and walked into the hall.

I knew our little conversation was lame and embarrassing, but I thought I escaped before Julie caught on to that fact. I was highly aware of how far she outclassed me. Julie was more attractive and popular

Courage, Love and the Meaning of Christmas

than I'd ever be. I was just another one of those guys that dreams way above his level. At least if I really was a loser, at least I had spoken, if only briefly and idiotically, to my dream girl. I bet most other losers have never done that!

Night fell early in winter and I walked home in the dark. Snow fell in flurries and I tucked my chin deeper into my parka's collar to keep the wind from working its way inside.

I replayed my interaction with Julie over and over through my mind, and was surprised to observe that I enjoyed the memory. Despite its flaws, I found myself feeling more satisfied and complete than I could remember.

What if Julie is my meaning of life? I wondered. Whether that made any sense or not, I couldn't write it in my paper. My professor would never understand.

At home, I tried to read, but couldn't focus. I couldn't keep Julie's face out of my mind or her voice out of my ears. "I think so," I heard her say over and over. "Okay, bye," she repeated endlessly while my mind's eye took in her blonde hair, bright eyes and the corner of her mouth.

"This is ridiculous," I told myself, but try as I might to avoid it, my thoughts kept drifting back to images of Julie and I cross-country skiing together, stopping in beautiful, deserted glades where she wrapped her arms around my neck and nibbled gently at my ear. I could feel her warm breath as she whispered my name and taste her soft lips as she pressed them against mine.

Finally, I gave up and shut my textbook, sliding it to the back of the desk. I kicked off my shoes and pulled my ski boots from the closet. I closed the door to my room long enough to grab my skis and poles leaning against the wall behind it, then headed outside to my car.

Five minutes later, I locked the car at the mouth of Green Canyon, clipped into my ski bindings, and started up the snow-covered road into the dark canyon alone.

5 Outside In

Three miles later, I lay in a clearing, eyes shut, lying flat on my back in the soft new snow. My coat lay unzipped and my chest rose and fell as I gasped for breath. Beads of sweat ran across my forehead and soaked into my hair.

As my heart rate slowed, I opened my eyes. Tiny, white snowflakes fell through the cold December air, landing silently on my hot face. They melted and ran in cool drops into my eyes and ears. I didn't lift my glove to wipe them away.

Plumes of warm steam rose into the air above my face with every exhalation, rising to join the low clouds that blocked the moon and stars and black winter night sky from view. I had skied hard, stepping forward on one ski and letting it glide several inches before bringing the other foot forward, and pushing hard with my poles.

It always worked for me before. The exertion of skiing uphill, the snow, the trees, the canyon walls and the breeze that sighed between them had a way of sucking all the pressure out from inside me. Of blowing the inner noise gently back down the canyon where it would soak into the deeply-rooted mountains or float away into the distant atmosphere.

In the silence left behind, I would find the peace. I would let the quiet stillness of nature seep into my soul. I would breathe in the cool, fresh air and burn it throughout the cells of my body. I would go back to my car with a fresh perspective, relaxed, breathing easily, smiling again and ready to take on another day.

Tonight, for the first time, it had failed. I skied hard for three miles, trying to work out all the stress and escape my distractions, but I felt no different than when I left the car over an hour ago. It was my own fault, I admitted.

I could have chosen an easy topic for my paper. I could have finished it a week ago. I could have found a less intimidating girl to have a crush on. I could just be satisfied with feeling a little stress and forget about finding peace in the middle of finals week. I could have...well, no, I couldn't.

I don't know when I first made the decision, I don't believe there was ever a specific moment of choice. It just happened. Somewhere in the path of growing up, I grew determined to do things well, to feel good and enjoy my life, to reach for the best and let nothing stop me or keep me down.

I never even realized I had made that decision until I began noticing the patterns of choices in my life. By that time the concept had rooted itself too deeply into my mind and heart and there was no turning back.

Of course this path wasn't always easy. In fact, it usually wasn't. Sometimes I wished I could just let go of my high hopes and expectations, but even when I opened my hand, they would not fall.

Courage, Love and the Meaning of Christmas

This left me standing somewhere in the gap between glory and failure, never quite reaching either side, always sprinting toward success and satisfaction, and away from fear and failure. Sometimes I felt choked, suffocated by self-induced pressure and my longing for unreached or unreachable goals.

When the pressure built up inside, I went outside. Soon the outside worked its way inside. Inside out and outside in, I finally felt like myself again.

But not tonight. Tonight the realization that I would never gain what I wanted most – Julie – had made me question whether I would ever feel truly satisfied. Before this realization, I had an impossible dream. After this obvious yet discouraging epiphany, I had nothing left worth dreaming about.

On top of everything else, I had to conclude a paper about the meaning of life. The very title irritated me now. I was seriously tempted to start over with a new topic, but with less than 48 hours left and other tests to study for, that was not an option.

At least in forty-eight hours it would be over, for better or worse. In two days I would pack up and head home for the Christmas holidays. I could sort everything out then. I could put everything behind me and start over.

Five minutes passed and the cold grew uncomfortable. I zipped up my coat and folded my arms across my chest. I wasn't ready to leave. I hadn't found my peace.

When I was young, I used to lay on the grass after school, staring up at the sky, looking for something above the high clouds. I used to sense God up there and imagined Him looking down at me, watching my thoughts and actions curiously as if wondering what I would think or do next. I always pictured Him like my grandfather, only with a flowing white beard and a sort of patient longing in his expression.

"Dear God," I whispered in a barely-audible voice. Even knowing I was utterly alone didn't make it comfortable to pray out loud. "Thanks for this beautiful canyon. Thanks for my family and friends and all my blessings and opportunities." I paused and searched for the next words, then half thought, half whispered them. *I'm sure everything will work out just fine, it always does...* "but could You give me a little hand? Maybe help me finish this paper, help me figure out the meaning of life?" *And help me forget about Julie, too, maybe. Maybe have one nice talk with her, and then get over her and get on with my life.* "Or whatever's best. Thanks again for everything. In Jesus' name, amen."

I lay there for a minute longer, looking for some indication that my prayer had reached heaven, then shivered and stood up. I clipped my boots into the ski bindings and took my first gliding steps down the canyon.

The narrow mountain walls to either side and low cloud ceiling above created the impression of skiing through a dim tunnel. I kept one foot a few inches in front of the other for balance as I sped quickly down a steep section of trail, my skis rattling over icy bumps beneath the new powder. When the canyon floor leveled out, I slipped into an easy step-glide, step-glide rhythm.

Maybe *that* was the meaning of life. You can't avoid the ups and downs, but when the downs come, just try not to fall and keep going until you warm up again.

I had given up on the idea that most of life can feel meaningful, but I desperately wanted to prove myself wrong. I wanted to discover the secret I had missed, something universally worth living for.

What I did not yet understand was that no one can just tell you the meaning of life. If someone had been waiting for me at the car and explained the whole thing, I wouldn't have understood.

Some things you have to experience for yourself to comprehend and appreciate. In hindsight, I see that my prayer did, in fact, reach heaven, and the experiences that would eventually teach me all I had asked for lay just around the corner.

6 Law of the Jungle

I got home around two a.m. and found my roommate Ben asleep on the couch. I picked up the remote and switched off the television, then found Ben's coat laying on the floor and draped it over him. He made a sound something between a snore and a snort but didn't wake up.

I went to my room and fell asleep without setting my alarm, and woke up after ten the next morning to continue working on my paper at the computer lab. I finally settled on the conclusion that "life is hard – live it anyway." Everyone agreed on the inevitability of suffering and confusion, but meaning is guaranteed to no one.

It wasn't great, but it was something. Just the thought of finishing the paper brought such relief that I gave up on finding the answer I once hoped for.

Around five o'clock, I printed out my latest draft and walked home for some dinner before Ski dropped by to pick me up and study at the library again. He pounded on the apartment door three times, then opened it and ran up the stairs three steps at a time into the living room.

"Hey, Ben," he said in a cheery tone, "ya just gonna sit and watch TV all night?" Tormenting my slightly overweight, couch-potato roommate was Ski's favorite activity whenever he paid us a visit. I had met Ben the day before classes began when I moved into the apartment. I met Ski the next day in philosophy, and Ben added the class a few days later. An entertaining circus of egos and intellects began immediately.

"Yep," Ben answered without looking away from the screen.

"Well at least you could sit on the other side of the couch. I've noticed this side sinks down a lot lower than the other side."

Ben looked up momentarily, annoyed. Ski smiled, seeing that he had found a sensitive spot. Ben looked away, then stood up and walked to the fridge for a soda.

"Hey Spencer!" Ski shouted toward my room, "You're not gonna believe this! I just saw Ben exercising! You told me he never did that!"

I walked into the living room with my coat and backpack. "Ready?" I asked Ski. I had long since given up telling Ski to go easy on Ben. Any kind of reaction from anyone at all only added fuel to the fire, and the only solution was to stop talking and walk away.

Ski was the most sarcastic person I had ever met, but I liked him anyway. His sarcasm probably had something to do with his upbringing. His parents were wealthy and distant. Rather than raising him themselves, they had depended on nannies and boarding schools. After graduating from high school, he finally had enough. Instead of accepting the full-ride scholarships offered to him by several Ivy League schools, he informed his parents that he would plan his own life from then on. "If you decline Harvard," they asked puzzledly, "where will you go?"

"Utah!" Ski answered randomly. And so he did. During the next three years, he only went home three or four times. At first,, he expected some kind of reaction to his first bid for independence, perhaps an argument about his choices or a new tension in their relationship, but found nothing more than an occasional confused expression on his parents' faces.

"It's funny that it never occurred to me," he told me one of the few times we spoke about his home life, "that we never had a relationship to begin with."

When I probed further, asking how he felt about all that, he slipped back into his playful, sarcastic mode and wouldn't give a straight answer. I finally gave up and accepted him the way he was, playing along when I felt like it and ignoring him the rest of the time.

"Where you guys going?" asked Ben, anxious not to be left out.

Ben's past was the exact opposite of Ski's. His father was his best friend, and vice versa. Together, they had won the state high school science fair two years in a row.

After listening to so many stories about his father's accomplishments, I once made the mistake of asking him a question. "Yeah," I said, "but what do you guys do for fun?"

What I got was a 40-minute rant about how much fun they had together, but it wasn't anything I recognized as a good time. They would sit at the table after dinner, for example, and create and solve geometry problems.

"What's the circumference of the earth?" his father would quiz.

"That's easy, dad – twenty-four thousand, four hundred fifty-two miles! Roughly a thousand miles per time zone."

"Easy, eh? Well what if you tied a string all the way around the world and then raised it an inch? How big of a gap would the ends of the string leave?"

Then they pulled out their pencils and protractors and calculated the answer. "Got it!" Ben would declare, pretending not to notice that his father had found the answer first.

"Now add that much string in to complete the loop," his father would continue. "Then pinch the string and lift. How high does the string go when you pull it tight against the other side of the world?"

And on and on and on they went. And on and on and on Ben went, telling me story after story after story. I was fascinated at how boring it all sounded, but even that fascination soon wore thin and I learned not to ask Ben questions unless I had somewhere I needed to go within the next few minutes.

Ben was a very friendly person, but all of his father's attention and praise had gone to his head, and now all his relationships seemed to be an effort to fit in socially while convincing everyone to accept his superiority over them – not a very endearing combination.

So when Ben asked where we were going, I had mixed feelings about telling him about our study session. One more person to look up answers would help, but there were costs to pay. My momentary hesitation was all Ski needed to take over.

Courage, Love and the Meaning of Christmas

"For a ride in Spencer's new car," he answered.

"Really? Why didn't you tell me you got a new car?" Ben asked. I raised one eyebrow at him and waited. It didn't take long.

"Where are you guys *really* going?"

"Study session," I answered.

"Philosophy? Why didn't you guys tell me?" Ben knew philosophy was the only class Ski and I had together. Now he became the picture of energy as he bounded to his room to grab his coat and pack while simultaneously trying to tie his shoelaces. Ski looked at me as if annoyed that I had let Ben in on our study session, but we both knew there would be significantly less work with him along. Ben's life consisted of television, studying, and chattering away while trying to act like one of the guys. We could stand him being around as long as we didn't get too much at once. Unfortunately for us, "too much" didn't take long to add up.

We reached the library after a fifteen-minute walk through the falling snow, listening to Ben chatter the whole way despite his huffing and puffing while trying to keep up as we walked up the hill to campus. Once inside the study room that Ski had reserved until midnight, the three of us shed our coats and spread our books and notes across the table.

Ben actually enjoyed tests. It gave him a chance to show off his high scores. I didn't understand how, after all this time, he could still expect everyone to fawn over him, pat him on the back, and want to be his friend because of it. So it almost surprised me when he began to complain now. "Why do we have to have finals, anyway?" he whined.

It *almost* surprised me, but not quite. I quickly saw that he was only trying to create a club of common opinion once Ski and I added our complaints, but we both knew better than to join in.

"The law of the jungle," Ski answered instead.

Ben and I looked at him. "What are you talking about?" Ben asked. Whenever he didn't understand something, he liked to make it sound like it hadn't been explained clearly, like it was someone else's fault. Whenever he caught on quickly to a concept in class, he raised his hand and commented on it just so everyone would know he understood. He either didn't notice or didn't care that even the professor was getting annoyed and trying to ignore his raised hand.

"The law of the jungle. You know — only the strong survive," Ski answered.

"Excuse me, but I fail to see the connection." Ben knew all too well that he had bought his way in to our group by looking up answers in advance, and knowing his security, he showed no qualms about taking the liberty to act obnoxious now.

"It wasn't in the text, Ben," Ski retorted. He never bothered to mask his feelings about Ben's self-centered attitude, or about anything else, for that matter. "But if you'll take your nose out of your books for a moment, you'll find it everywhere around you."

"Well not only the strong survive finals, you know," Ben countered. "What about cheaters, or hard workers, or students who avoid all the hard classes?"

"Don't you get it?" Ski asked, shaking his head in mock disbelief at Ben's obtuseness. "I never said you had to be smart. Lions aren't the only animals left in the jungle."

"Technically," Ben began to object, "lions don't live in the jungle...."

"Shut up," Ski commanded, "we know."

"Technically," I began, trying to shift the focus of the conversation before this little tournament of egos got out of control and I didn't get the answers for the study guide, "we came here for a study session, not a pointless argument."

"Technically," Ski continued, ignoring my redirect, "we have to have finals to maintain the status quo. By flunking out the dummies, academia retains its prestige and the brainiacs retain their power."

"Technically," Ben began again.

"Shut up," Ski cut him off.

Ben's feelings looked momentarily hurt, but he continued anyway. "You still didn't respond to my objection about cheaters."

"Yes I did," Ski retorted. "They're the jackals. But the lions are still king of the...savannah."

"So what you're saying," I interrupted again, attempting to bring the debate to a close so we could get on with looking up study guide answers, "is that unless we're smart, then our professors really are trying to eliminate us?"

"Spencer," Ski answered, cocking his head to one side and looking tired, "this study guide is six pages long. Can you think of a better way?"

"Oh," chirped Ben cheerily, instantly forgetting the brief argument, "I've already finished three pages."

Ski and I smiled at how little work we'd each have to do.

"As much as they'd like to," Ski sighed, "no professor will ever eliminate Ben."

7 Wish

I glanced up from our notes and saw Julie gazing in through the room's glass door. I smiled a little and waved. She smiled back and opened the door.

"Hi Julie," I said. Out of the corner of my eye, I saw Ben's jaw drop as I greeted the girl we had all watched and talked about all semester long.

"Hey," she said, looking directly at me, "I finished my paper."

"I bet that feels good." I felt like a million dollars. This was too good to be true. She acted like she knew who I was and it suddenly felt easy, natural, to talk to her.

"It does," she admitted, then asked, "Why didn't you tell me your paper is getting published?!"

Ben's jaw dropped far enough that I wondered if it would cause permanent tissue damage. I instantly understood what had happened. Ski had struck up a conversation with her outside of class and embellished it with his typical inventions. I never understood how he could keep from bursting out laughing as I struggled to figure out what lies I had to work around.

"Well, it's not official yet. Personally, I don't think it's that good. Would you like to join our study session?" I asked, changing the subject as quickly as possible.

"Sure," she answered. "Ski told me about it yesterday. Hi, Ski." Julie walked around the room and sat down between Ski and me.

Once again, I felt grateful for Ski's audacity. While the rest of us were gawking and dreaming about Julie, he had actually walked up to her, introduced himself, and invited her to our study session, all without telling us so that when she arrived, the effect would be even more dramatic. Ski's patience was sometimes as extreme as his usual impatience, and now I caught him watching our reactions closely for the payoff.

A few other students came and went and the clock on the wall read eleven thirty when we finished answering all the study guide questions and copying each other's notes. I had never enjoyed studying so much. For the first time, I wasn't anxious to finish.

"Anyone in the mood for waffles and ice cream?" Ski asked. I knew he was only doing me a favor by trying to keep Julie around for a little longer. I wouldn't forget this.

"I've been sitting around all day long," Julie answered. "I don't dare eat again."

"I know what you mean," I said, "I'm so restless—we should go cross-country skiing. It's beautiful at night." It was worth a try, I thought. Audacity. Law of the jungle. Only the strong survive.

"That sounds fun," Julie said, "but I don't have skis."

"I know someone who works at the Outdoor Rec Center, and I'm pretty sure he'd be willing to get us a pair of skis tonight." I wasn't about to give up easily.

Julie looked from me to Ski and back at me. All semester long I had avoided eye contact. Now I couldn't look away.

"Okay, sounds great!"

Adam wasn't thrilled about leaving his date to unlock the Rec Center and get us skis, but it meant three pages of notes that he would never have looked up himself. "See what I mean?" he asked with another reverse-wink as I handed him the copies. "Everything falls right into my lap."

Ski and Ben decided to go for a midnight snack. "I've never tried cross-country skiing," Ben had begun to say, but Ski cut him off.

"You're hungry," he insisted, gripping Ben's shoulder firmly. "Let's go."

Julie and I clipped into our bindings and started up the trail in Green Canyon a little after midnight.

"Do you cross country much?" I asked, trying to make conversation.

"I used to," Julie answered, "but I don't know many trails around here."

I found myself in pure heaven! Here I stood alone with the girl of my dreams and I knew enough ski trails to keep us busy for months. I could keep her interest by bringing my camp stove along and cooking gourmet meals on the trail along with star charts to memorize the constellations at night. I could bring her home for hot chocolate or spaghetti or even a movie. And all the while, I would stare into her beautiful blue eyes and....

"How long have you known Ski?" Julie asked.

"Just a few months," I answered casually. "We met in class, in fact. But we hang out a lot."

"What kinds of things does he like to do?"

"Oh, I think he'd have fun no matter what he was doing."

"We'll all have to get together again after finals," she suggested.

It grew quickly clear where Julie's real interests lay. I would have to find a new meaning of life, but at least my wish had come true for tonight.

Courage, Love and the Meaning of Christmas

8 To Be Great

Ski and I agreed to meet for lunch the next day. I picked up an enchilada at the food court and found an empty table. Ski spotted me and walked over.

"How'd it go?" he asked.

"We agreed on a June wedding."

"Wow, that good, eh?"

"No, not really," I answered. "You gonna eat something?"

"Yeah, it's coming. What really happened?"

"She only had one thing on her mind."

Ski paused for a moment. "You look serious. Are you serious?"

"Totally. But it's not what you're thinking."

"What, then?" Ski asked, glancing toward the food court entrance.

"You."

Ski looked back at me. "What do you mean?"

"I mean all she's really interested in is you. Wants to know what you like to do, wants to get together after finals."

A pizza delivery guy walked in and looked hopelessly around the crowded room. Ski stood up and waved him over.

"Hmm," he said after paying for the pizza and opening the box. "I'm not sure I could go for the perfect type."

"You might as well give it a shot," I said, wondering if he only said that to be nice, to avoid gloating. I was touched that he would skip his usual sarcasm for a topic that I might have found sensitive. "You never know till you try. And at least I'll be nearby to look at her."

Ski took two slices of pizza from the box and folded one over the top so all the toppings were sandwiched in the middle. I admired the way he did everything differently, his own way. Ski was anything but traditional, and it seemed liberating.

It was too late to revise my philosophy paper, but I was curious. Maybe Ski would have something helpful to tell me about the meaning of life. I didn't care about the paper anymore, but I would still like to find an answer to the question.

We ate in silence for a minute or two, then I asked, "So, Ski, you seem to have opinions on just about everything. What would you say is the meaning of life?"

Ski laughed. "You mean that law of the jungle thing?" He chewed and laughed again. "I just made that up last night 'cause Ben was annoying me." He grinned, remembering how much he had enjoyed winning the argument. "But let's see. The meaning of life? Yes, it's to be great. I'm sure of it."

"Oh yeah?" I asked, intrigued. Ski's ideas were unlike anything I had found in any dense, dead philosopher's writings. "You mean like by achieving a lot and changing the world?"

"Not necessarily. Most people think that way, but that's just because of competition, which is a ridiculous substitute for true greatness." Ski took another bite of pizza, then continued talking with his mouth full. "See, to be great in everybody else's eyes, you just have to be better than they are. It's just a race, a game. It's fun if you're a good player, but everyone else loses. That reminds me of Ben – he's such a loser because he tries so hard to be a winner.

"Me," he continued, "I don't care what anyone else thinks, so for me, to be great would be to please myself as well as possible."

"And how do you do that?" I asked. I had entirely forgotten about the paper now — I wanted to understand this for myself.

"By doing whatever I feel like. Usually, I just feel annoyed by stupid people, so I put them in their place."

"You mean like Socrates? He was always putting people in their place and everybody thinks he was great."

"No, I wouldn't want to be like him — that's different, he's not my hero. After all, he drank poison rather than letting his friends buy his way out of prison. Thought he had a duty to obey some stupid law. Why should I suffer because of someone else's idiotic ideas? I would have just paid off the guards, gotten out of jail, and enjoyed a refreshing drink of cold lemonade on the beach. I hear they've got some really nice beaches in Greece."

"And that makes life worthwhile — just doing what you feel like?" I hoped he was right, I hoped he would convince me. I sensed that there was some key here that might help to free me from my own stresses and fears and limitations and let me get on with my life without it feeling like such a constant struggle.

Ski continued chewing his pizza while looking down at the table and thinking for a moment, just to make sure.

"What else is there?" he finally answered.

9 Split

The next day passed slowly. I stayed up late studying for the philosophy exam and took it before noon. Ben finished his test first, but sat in his seat pretending to review his answers until Ski and I finished.

As we walked out of the room, there wasn't much left to say.

"Enjoy your break," I said, giving a single wave goodbye.

"Are you going home for Christmas?" Ben asked Ski.

"Not right away," Ski answered. "I'm gonna leave this prison behind and head down to Mexico to lie on the beach for a week first."

"Really?" Ben asked.

"Gonna drink some lemonade there?" I asked.

"Yeah," he answered, remembering our conversation about Socrates and ignoring Ben. "Exactly."

The thought of warm sand and sunshine felt good. I considered asking if he needed company, but the savings from my part-time job on campus would barely pay for the gas to get there. Besides, I knew he wasn't really going. Still, I couldn't help wishing the trip was real. That seemed like the perfect way to practice doing what I felt like.

"What about you?" Ben asked. At first, I was surprised to find him interested in anything but himself, but quickly recognized the setup — he only wanted a chance to tell us about his own plans once his turn came.

"Oh, home for a few days and then a week or so at my grandma's in Wyoming," I answered.

Ben waited a few seconds to see if anyone would ask about his plans, then volunteered the information as if someone had. "Yeah, I'm going home, too," he said. "My dad wants me to help debug a handwriting-recognition and personality-analyzing program he wrote."

I could tell that Ski was impressed. So was I. It actually sounded interesting. But we both knew better than to give any indication. Any recognition at all would send Ben into a lengthy explanation that neither of us had the patience to endure.

Julie stepped out the door of the classroom just in time to stop Ben from taking advantage of the momentary silence and launching into his explanation. "Hey guys," she said, smiling. "I'm sure glad that's over. Anybody wanna go for hot chocolate?"

Ben looked torn. "I've got another final in ten minutes," he said apologetically.

"That's what you get for taking twenty-two credits," Ski answered.

"What about you, Spence?"

I could think of nothing else I'd rather do, but I knew better than to cling to my old, futile dreams. I also remembered the favor Ski had done me last night by making sure Julie and I got a chance to be alone, and decided to repay the favor now. "Sorry," I answered sincerely, "I can't. I've got to pack and head home. My family's expecting me for dinner tonight."

"Then I guess it's just us," Julie said to Ski. She tried to hide the excitement in her voice and eyes, but it shone through and didn't escape me.

"Merry Christmas," Ski said, somewhat intensely, nodding toward me. I thought I caught a subtle message encoded in his piercing glance, but could not decipher it. I just assumed it was the closest Ski could come to expressing how he felt about our friendship. This assumption was reinforced by recalling that Ski, a dedicated cynic by nature, never wished anyone a 'Merry Christmas', said 'Have a nice day' nor expressed any other courteous but trite phrase.

"Same to you," I answered, returning a casual nod.

"Merry Christmas," Ben added. I had forgotten he was even there. With nothing left to say, we turned and walked away in different directions.

10 Do What You Feel

I packed my things quickly and loaded the car. I had nothing left to do but eat lunch and head home to Orem, which waited two hours to the south. I looked through the cupboards for something to make, but didn't feel like cooking. Instead, I just grabbed some granola bars that I kept on hand for ski trips and washed them down with a glass of milk. "Doing what I feel," I thought to myself.

Outside, I started the car and let it run to warm up and defrost the windshield. It would feel good to get home. I could relax there, and unlike being at school, I wouldn't be surrounded by teachers and strangers, I wouldn't be judged and evaluated every step of the way.

And I was tired. Tired of staying up studying, tired of work, tired of thinking. It was high time I took a real break.

As I thought about the drive home, a strange feeling washed over me. I suddenly didn't want to go. It occurred to me that home might not be the best place in the world to take a break right now. My little sisters

Courage, Love and the Meaning of Christmas

would pile all over me and never let me rest. I loved them, of course, loved asking them questions, listening to their stories and playing with them, but for the moment, I only wanted to kick back and veg out, not play and talk with them non-stop.

Then there was Dad. He'd expect me to find a job for the break, though I'd waste half my vacation looking for a seasonal job that would let me off during Christmas to go to Grandma's. No, now that I thought about it, I definitely didn't feel like going home. I needed rest and enough time to de-stress, not new challenges.

Instead, another destination came to mind, and with it, a calm feeling of peace settled deep into my heart. Stress and fatigue faded from my mind as if I was suddenly viewing them from a great distance or a far-removed place in time.

And that was enough, the decision was made. I put the car in reverse and backed out of the parking space. When I reached the street, I didn't turn west toward the highway and home, but east toward the canyon instead. I knew just the place where I could make myself comfortable, enjoy plenty of peace and quiet, and have no forced responsibilities. This year, I was heading for Wyoming and Grandma's early and alone.

"Doing what I feel," I told myself again.

11 Annetta

I pulled off the highway three hours later in Amber, Wyoming. Grandma's place stood five miles north of here, away from the dozen or so businesses and the cluster of homes in a small town that time forgot. I thought of it that way partly because it lay in one of the few remaining blank spots of every cellular-phone-coverage map, and partly because everyone and everything seemed so old fashioned - which probably endured because the lack of internet and cable TV (unless you had a satellite dish) prevented social media and other services from accelerating the pace of life to modern, breakneck speeds.

Until now, I hadn't thought at all about dropping in early and unexpectedly or how I would explain why I came. Not that it would cause any problem. I knew Grandma would welcome me any time and be excited to see me early. It would feel nice to have a little time together before the crowds of aunts, uncles and cousins showed up.

Still, she would also ask why I had come early, and I wanted to give her a better answer than just that I felt like it. It was the truth, but I should at least decide how to phrase it.

I saw a café called Becca's Diner next to the highway truck stop and decided to pull in for a bite to eat and a minute to think. When I pulled into the empty parking lot and shut off the engine, the ensuing and absolute silence surprised me. It was my first reminder of the pleasantly peaceful atmosphere of this small town.

I walked into the diner and took a seat at the bar. The rest of the room was deserted and I began to feel a little foolish, wondering if the kitchen was even open. Why did I need to stop, anyway? Five miles of road would have given me plenty of time to plan out a few sentences. I nearly stood up and walked back outside when a waitress stepped out of the kitchen and walked toward me.

She was slender, around 5'5" and perhaps 22 years old. Her light brown hair hung in a pony tail to the nape of her neck. She wore no make up and a few light freckles dotted her nose and cheeks. Her name tag said Annetta. Something about the way she walked seemed carefree and light, and she began to smile the moment our eyes met. "Hi," she said.

Although I had spent many weeks in Amber over the past several years, I had always spent them with my family and never met anyone my own age. Chances were low that this girl and I would have much in common, but she seemed friendly and I decided to stay and at least make an acquaintance in case I got bored later on, which would probably happen sooner than later.

"Hi, Annetta," I replied.

Her eyebrows raised a little, startled that I knew her name, then she smiled again as she remembered her name tag. "Can I get you something?" she asked.

"I think so," I answered. "What are you serving at this time of day?"

She leaned over the hardwood bar toward me on her elbows. "I was just about to warm up the grill. You can have anything on the menu."

I picked up a menu from the counter and scanned through the choices. I didn't really feel like eating just now, but I would feel dumb just walking out without ordering something. "What do you recommend?"

"Everything on there's delish," Annetta answered, looking me steadily in the eye. She leaned farther over the bar toward me to read the menu and make her recommendation. Suddenly the word lemonade caught my eye, and before I could stop myself, "How about a glass of lemonade?" I asked.

Annetta smiled slightly as if wondering whether or not to take me seriously. "Okay," she said. "One refreshing lemonade for a hot winter day."

I almost began to blush as she walked back into the kitchen to mix up some lemonade, but she had looked amused. Anyway, who cares? I felt no need to impress anyone here. *Law of the jungle*, I told myself. *Do what I feel.*

I glanced around the empty dining room, noticing the old booths covered in red vinyl and an antique juke box against the far wall. From the kitchen came sounds of running water and cracking ice, a wooden spoon against a glass pitcher, then the sounds of Annetta's shoes walking back toward me. "Here you go," she said, setting my lemonade on the counter.

I gave her a smile in response, she smiled back, and I noticed what a terrific smile she had, full of confidence and casual energy. In her simple, down-to-earth, small-town way, she was a rather attractive girl. Then another thought jumped into my mind, and before I could dismiss it, "Hey Annetta," I said, "I'm pretty much alone here until my family shows up next week. Wanna do something sometime?"

Annetta's eyes widened slightly and she looked startled. "Perhaps," she answered cautiously. Her smile faded a little and I sensed a guarded distance appear between us. She probably had obnoxious country boys in here all the time trying to pick up on her. "What did you have in mind?"

"Actually," I admitted, "I hadn't thought that far ahead. I've always just spent the holidays north of town with my family. What is there to do around here?"

"Who's your family?" Annetta inquired.

"Sophia Rasmussen is my grandma."

"Sophie's your grandmother?" Annetta asked, looking surprised again. Her eyes lit up once more and the distance faded. "The high school's putting on a play tonight at six – Fiddler on the Roof. I live just over the river. You can pick me up here."

"Sounds great, I'll be here at a quarter to."

"I'll be waiting."

I couldn't wait to get back to school and tell Ski how well his philosophy worked. In a single day, I had learned how to do what I felt and it seemed to be working out great so far. I took a long drink of lemonade and tried to think of something cool to say, but nothing came to mind. A tiny bell jingled as the first customer of the evening wandered through the door, a rugged-looking man with a mustache and cowboy hat. The man sat down at the far end of the bar and I began feeling self-conscious. I decided to leave before saying something dumb. "My name's Spencer, by the way."

"Well it's a pleasure to meet you, Spencer." Annetta reached over the bar and shook my hand. She held on just a moment longer than normal.

"You, too, Annetta. I'll see you tonight." I pulled a handful of change from my pocket, placed it on the counter, and walked outside.

"Who was that?" I heard the man's voice inquire as the door closed slowly behind me.

12 Mansions & Memories

Ever since I was small, Grandma's home always felt magic. The roof peaked steeply with a tower over the spiral staircase that led all the way up to the attic above the third floor. Its imposing silhouette and many rooms provided plenty of space for my imagination to run wild.

Giant old cottonwoods stood leaflessly around the house throughout winter, and whether they creaked slowly back and forth in the wind or stood eerily still, they added to the mystery, to the feeling that a fairy tale had occurred in this very place, and not long ago.

I turned off the car near the back door and climbed the wooden staircase to the porch. The old wood creaked underfoot, but the porch had been swept clean and tidy. Long years of foot traffic had worn the wood smooth.

I paused to listen to that silence impossible to find anywhere except in the country. A near-tangible stillness hung in the air, clinging to the slight breeze, echoing the absence of the hum of traffic or any other sound of civilization. The silence and peace fell comfortably over wide fields of harvested corn and wheat like a thick down comforter.

The quiet calm created its own unique sense of time. In fact, time seemed to disappear altogether. As long as the chores had been finished, no rush or hurry could exist in a place like this where one day blended so pleasantly into the next. I found it impossible to keep that peace from overflowing from the fields and pouring inside myself, spilling all the way down to my toes, filling me with a deep serenity I had never experienced anywhere else.

A pair of pheasant darted across the driveway and disappeared into

Courage, Love and the Meaning of Christmas

the short cornstalks at the edge of the fields as I leaned comfortably against a round wooden pillar on the porch. After a few deep breaths of cool, dry air, I turned and opened the door, which had likely not been locked for the last decade.

"Grandma?" I called into the house. "It's Spencer!" I paused to listen for squeaking floor boards somewhere in the house. "Anybody home?" I shouted again. No answer.

If the peaceful countryside had a powerful effect on me, this home's touch felt even stronger. Everything seemed as familiar as my family's home in Orem where I spent sixteen long years of my life. Something about the old wood and new paint, the wood burning stoves, and the generations who were born and died here, gave it substance and made it feel more real on some deep level that I did not begin to understand.

"Anybody home?" I called again, stepping through the kitchen and living room. At the base of the spiral stairway, a large, white, wooden ball a little smaller than a basketball adorned the end of the handrail. My grandfather had added this touch when I was a child and I used to look into it and tell stories as if it were a crystal ball.

The nostalgia of my younger years flooded over me as I suddenly realized that I now stood in the future I had imagined so often as a child. Of course the present had little in common with the fantasies I invented then. As it turns out, this crystal ball only had power to look backward in time.

I walked upstairs and down the hall to a small bedroom with two beds where my older brother and I had stayed from time to time. The thin crack still ran through the middle of the door and the floorboards creaked beneath my feet in the hallway. This same sound would warn me when Grandpa was coming to wake me up when I spent summers here before I turned ten. I would wake up before he walked into the room and put his large hand on my shoulder, but I would pretend to be dreaming anyway.

"Hey, City Boy," he used to whisper. "Ya wanna help me squeeze some fresh cow juice for Grandma?"

I'd roll over slowly and stretch, then pull back the thick quilts and get dressed before going out to the barn to help milk.

"Nothing like gettin' up at the crack o' dawn, is there?" he'd always say as I walked groggily into the barn. Of course he'd have been up for an hour or two already doing other chores, but it made me feel like a real rancher, and I still remember the love in his eyes as I beamed back at him wordlessly.

I suddenly felt the overwhelming urge to run outside to the barn and start milking again, to reach back to the past and pull myself into its comforting arms, but the cows were gone, along with the rest of the animals and Grandpa himself. Now others farmed the land and paid enough rent to take care of all Grandma's needs. Grandpa passed away a year ago last September, just as the aspen and cottonwood leaves began to glow their bright yellows and reds in the nearby foothills. I missed him.

The barn now only held Grandpa's old truck and other odd items that would probably spend the rest of eternity in storage there. I walked back downstairs and outside anyway, suddenly unable to bear the emptiness of the house.

Wandering into the barn, I found an ax leaning up against the wall near the woodpile. I pulled off my coat and set to chopping sections of logs into pieces that would fit into the wood burning stoves. The air felt cold At first,, but swinging the heavy ax warmed me quickly. The activity cleared my mind and I soon felt calm again.

After ten or fifteen minutes, I stopped and replaced the ax. By now, sweat ran down my forehead and the cold air bit at my throat and lungs with each deep breath. I walked to the doorway and leaned against the rough wood and old red paint with my hands shoved deep into my pockets.

Then, for the second time today, a feeling of deep peace and love washed over and through me. I hadn't felt so good or relaxed for months, maybe years. I breathed deeply and wondered what it was that made me so wonderfully happy yet still sent a tear spilling down my cold cheek.

13 Grandma

A car pulled up and stopped in front of the house, gravel crunching beneath its tires. I picked up my coat and walked inside for a drink of water, and as I drained the glass, Grandma walked through the front door. I set the glass on the counter and walked into the living room to meet her.

The sight that met my eyes startled me. Grandma looked older than I had ever seen her. She moved slowly and carefully, her head hanging low. She was in her mid-seventies, but I had never really thought of her as old until right now. She always seemed so youthful, so energetic and

Courage, Love and the Meaning of Christmas

warm. The image of her I carried in my mind was of her holding hands with Grandpa, laughing together or singing around the old piano on Christmas Eve. I repressed the initial urge to run forward and shout "Surprise!" and paused in the doorway instead.

"Merry Christmas, Grandma," I said gently.

She started slightly and looked up. Suddenly a spark ignited in her eyes. "Spencer!" She stepped forward, her head up now, the old familiar energy restored. "You're early! Has your whole family come?" I breathed a little sigh of relief to see her back to her old self.

"Nope, just me, Gram." By this time our arms were around each other and squeezing tight. I breathed another sigh of relief as I noticed how hard she could still squeeze. Maybe she had only looked old for a moment. Maybe I had nothing to worry about.

"So," she said as she stepped back and looked me over. "What brings you here so early?"

I had forgotten all about planning my story — it seemed ridiculous now anyway. As long as it was the truth, it was good enough for Grandma.

"Actually, I just felt like it."

Grandma smiled at this and I watched warm tears well up in her eyes. "Well I certainly am happy to see you. Thank you for coming."

"I'm glad I did."

"You'll have to tell me all about your classes and friends." She emphasized 'friends' just enough to imply 'girlfriends' as well.

"There's not much to tell," I confessed. "But I do have a date tonight. We're going to the high school play."

"A date?" she asked, looking surprised. "Who's the lucky girl?"

"Her name's Annetta. She works at the diner by the highway."

"Oh, Annetta Hall — she is a very sweet girl. I didn't know you knew her," she said, knitting her brow slightly.

"Well, we just met, actually. I stopped there on my way through town. What do you know about her?"

"Oh, she's simply wonderful. You two will get along just fine. I imagine she'll rather enjoy having someone her age to talk to." Grandma looked at me thoughtfully for a moment, and I wondered if she was imagining Annetta and I as a couple.

"It's too bad," Grandma began, then stopped.

"What?" I asked curiously.

"Nothing," Grandma answered, waving off whatever she was about to say. "I shouldn't spoil anything by telling you what she can tell you better herself. By the way," she added, "does your family know you've come?" When I paused, she added, "I'll give them a call. You'd better get ready."

14 Courage

Annetta was nowhere to be seen through the glass windows of Becca's Diner as I pulled up outside a few minutes early. I sat in my car until a quarter to, then walked inside. I stepped up to the bar where I had ordered lemonade that afternoon and a lanky cook glanced up at me. He looked about 20 and his white apron seemed like it hadn't been washed for the last 500 greasy hamburgers. His cowboy boots echoed off the tile floor as he stepped toward me behind the bar.

"What kin I git ya?" he asked.

"Oh, I'm just waiting for Annetta," I answered. "Looks like she's not here yet."

The boy just stared back without responding. For a moment, I thought he hadn't understood, but then I noticed the way he glared at me. It seemed like a combination of sizing me up and staring me down. His eyes narrowed a bit and he pursed his lips off to one side. It felt like some kind of challenge, and I wondered if this was Annetta's boyfriend. That could explain Grandma's little secret that she hadn't told me. The boy gave no sign of talking, so I took the middle road and retreated without backing down.

I stared back steadily for a moment, giving no sign that I was even aware of the challenge, then looked around at the booths away from the bar and said, "I'll just wait for her over here."

"She ain't workin' tonight," the boy said flatly.

"Yeah," I said, "I know. We're going to the play in a few minutes." If this was my competition, I may as well get it out in the open. I took a seat across from the door, looked around the room, then out the window. In the reflection on the glass, I watched the door open and Annetta walk in and look around for me. I turned toward her just as the cook caught her eye.

"Hey, Netta," he said, slow and drawn out, as if he really meant to say, "Who is this guy? What's going on here?"

"Hey Jim," she answered casually, then saw me and walked over. "What's up, Spencer? Ya ready?"

"All set," I answered, standing up. I wondered what sort of waves my appearance was causing and what minor melodramas I might be stepping into.

"All right then," she said, tilting her head toward the door. "Let's go. Bye, Jim," she said as we walked past the bar. Jim didn't answer. I sensed his glare even after the door closed behind us.

Annetta had taken her light brown hair out of the pony tail and curled the ends under. Her tan sheepskin coat looked warm and new and like it had seen more time on Rodeo Drive than in the saddle. Her pastel-blue t-shirt, together with jeans and light hiking shoes, gave her a comfortable, down-to-earth look.

Annetta glanced up at me as we stepped off the curb and flashed a quick smile. *Wow,* I thought to myself, *she's really cute!* She didn't have Julie's perfect features and flawless skin, but I found her slender figure and simple, wholesome, girl-next-door appearance quite attractive.

With that thought, my old insecurities came rushing back. I felt intimidated. The old pressure to be cool, the need to impress her, and the fear that I'd say something stupid made it impossible to say anything at all. I wanted to be audacious and say, "You look great," but the words got stuck in my throat.

I pulled my car keys from my pocket and stepped toward the passenger door, still reaching for something to say.

"Let's walk," Annetta said. "It's only a couple blocks."

"Sounds great."

"So, what do you do, Spencer?" Annetta asked.

"I'm going to school at Utah State." I felt slightly relieved to have the silence broken.

"Really? What's your major?" she continued. Her voice was light and carefree. Everything about her felt alive and happy. She almost skipped as she walked.

"Um, it's English. But I'm looking into some other majors." I suddenly didn't like the sound of my own voice. It sounded drab and boring compared to her lively inflection.

"Really? Like what?"

"I don't know. I thought about philosophy for a little while, but I've sort of lost interest in it."

"Why?"

I looked over at Annetta. She met my gaze and waited for my answer as she skipped along next to me. "Um, I guess, just because I took this class and sort of realized that, um, that philosophers don't really know all that much."

"Oh," she simply replied.

"I mean, sure they know stuff," I continued, feeling a little defensive, "but it's like they're missing lots of stuff, too. Or like even if you study all those ideas, it doesn't really make that much difference in your life."

"Hmm," she said. I guess she was just making small talk. I shouldn't have given such a long answer to her question. I'd be more careful from now on. Before I could throw in a question of my own and change the subject and get her to do more of the talking, she asked, "So what *does* make a difference?"

"I don't know. That's sort of what I'm stuck on. What do you think?"

"Let's see," she replied, pausing momentarily. "I'd have to say... courage."

It didn't sound much like philosophy, but it caught my interest.

"Oh?" I asked, "How so?"

"Well," she explained, "if you have courage, then it changes not only what you do, but how you do it. It makes everything better."

I liked her idea instantly. I didn't know why, but it sounded right. As a matter of fact, it sounded more useful than anything I had studied all semester long.

"Where did you learn that?" I asked.

"I don't know," she answered. "Just figured it out somewhere along the way."

We crossed a small bridge and I saw the school just down the block.

"Would you say courage is the meaning of life?" I asked, wondering if I could resolve my whole question right here, one day too late for the paper assignment.

"I don't know if I'd go *that* far," Annetta answered. "but it probably adds some meaning to life."

"Well it sounds a lot more useful than existentialism or nihilism or any of that stuff."

"Yeah," Annetta answered. "I see what you mean now. Getting analytical and abstract about life doesn't automatically translate into meaningful actions and feelings. I thought Maslow's hierarchy of needs was pretty insightful, though, but that's more psychology than philosophy, isn't it?"

How did she know about Maslow? I began to realize that I didn't know the first thing about this girl.

"Did you just figure that out along the way, too?"

She laughed and answered, "No, got that one in school."

"Where'd you go?" I asked.

Courage, Love and the Meaning of Christmas

"San Diego State," she answered. "I just finished up this summer."

"Oh, yeah? What was your major?" I asked, relieved to note that our conversation was gaining some momentum and discover that perhaps we had more in common than I thought.

"Philosophy," she said, looking at me with one eyebrow raised playfully, then added, "Just kidding." She laughed a little and looked up toward the stars already beginning to appear in the evening sky, then down toward the darkening horizon. I watched her green eyes and they danced as she continued. "It was Liberal Arts & Sciences, so I got a little of everything. I like it that way."

"Yeah? Like what?" I asked.

Annetta thought for a moment, then looked me in the eye to answer casually. "Everything," she said. "I guess because awareness of anything makes it more interesting because you know how to appreciate it. Like biology and humanities and psychology. The more you know about them, the more exciting and meaningful everything becomes."

It wasn't just what Annetta said, but the way she said it that made her ideas feel fresh and interesting. Her underlying interest in the world spilled out with her ideas and flavored them like raspberry vinaigrette dressing poured over salad.

"What do you like about majoring in English?" Annetta asked.

I thought for a moment and didn't think of any profound answers. "I like it better than anything else I've found," I said.

"Why?" She wasn't going to let me off easy.

"I like the discussions we have about the readings," I answered, "and writing the papers, most of the time. It seems like analyzing stories and applying them to our own circumstances helps make more sense of life, sometimes."

"Always looking for the meaning of life, huh?"

"I guess so," I said. I had never thought of it that way before, but now the pattern seemed blatantly obvious.

"What have you found out about it so far?" Annetta asked. She looked me in the eye again and I could read her genuine curiosity about the topic. As long as she was interested in me and my thoughts, I guess it wasn't so bad for me to be doing most of the talking instead of her.

I hadn't found out anything useful in my philosophy paper, but maybe my old English papers held some clues. Dozens of ideas sprang to mind, but none of them conclusive, none of them could summarize the meaning of Meaning itself. "It seems to change for every character and situation," I finally answered, "Which would explain why everyone finds 'the meaning of life' so elusive."

"Hmm," Annetta thought out loud. "I think we're dealing with two different questions here. In the first place, there's the definition of the meaning of life, and then there's the application of it so life feels meaningful."

I nodded my head and wished we had had this conversation two months earlier before spending so much time in futile research for my paper.

"Now we just need some research questions."

"Like 'what makes life feel meaningful?'" I asked.

The street lamp above our heads flickered on and Annetta looked up and gave me a confident smile in response, without even nodding, as if the answer was too obvious to waste any words or energy on. I began to fall in love with the idea that our conversation could jump right past all the formalities, all the trivial details, all the banal observations, all the worrying about being good enough, and skip straight to the important, interesting, useful points.

The challenge of talking with Annetta reminded me of Ski, except that Annetta's discussions invited exploration while Ski instigated contests. A team effort rather than a battle of wits.

I also began to feel something I had hardly experienced since I was a child. It was the feeling of waking up early every morning and wondering what grand adventure I would discover that day. The anticipation of feeling the wind blow through my hair, of tasting the humid morning air in my lungs, the salty blood pumping through my veins as I ran. The impression that every door was open to me, that every barrier was nothing more than a playground toy to scramble over, that life was for living and every thought was a possibility.

I quickly recognized the basis of this new feeling - curiosity. Curiosity about every aspect of life opening my eyes wide to the world around me, opening my heart and mind to experience and understanding.

I had naturally known this curiosity as a child, but had largely, inadvertently abandoned it through neglect, through fears about whether or not I was accepted or good enough, and through a shortage of friends who understood why everything matters so much.

I had smothered it under the demands of keeping up with school and work and the expectations I felt from everyone around me. I had nearly forgotten how it felt and how much I loved and missed this

Courage, Love and the Meaning of Christmas

sensation. Now it all came rushing back, rising slowly into my mind like the surge of high tide creeping steadily up the beach, and my self-awareness surprised me.

As Annetta looked confidently up at me I felt like we shared a common bond, a secret pact that no one else could see or understand. I felt excited to get to know her better and perhaps figure out why this girl and the curiosity she awoke in me had begun to make life feel meaningful.

"Ya know what, Annetta?" I said, stopping as we reached the school parking lot. "I still don't know the first thing about you. Would you just start at the beginning or in the middle or anywhere and tell me all about yourself?"

"Hey," she answered, stopping to face me. "I don't know anything about you, either. When are you going to take your turn?"

"Right after you, I promise."

Annetta considered this for a moment, cocking her head to one side with her hair falling partly across her face, then assented. "Well, I suppose the middle is as good a spot to start as anywhere," she began.

"How do you know what's the middle?"

"As long as it's not the beginning or the end, it must be the middle," she explained. I nodded and she continued. "Winter is beautiful, but I prefer summer...."

I loved the chance this gave me to just look at her, to watch the way she walked and listen to the passion for life evident in her voice. I watched the sparkle in her bright green eyes and the way her lips moved over her teeth. I noticed the locals as they drove past us to park or walked in groups toward the door, the way they all craned their necks and stared to see the new guy walking with Annetta.

I bought a pair of tickets and we strolled into the auditorium. We sat off to one side and continued talking. Annetta had hardly begun her life summary when the pit orchestra began to play. We talked until the curtain rose and out walked Tevye to introduce the play.

15 Chemistry

During intermission, Annetta and I wandered through the high school's narrow halls, talking until half a dozen kids running and playing tag nearly knocked us over. We stepped into a classroom then, filled with lab tables and half-set-up test tube experiments.

We began our conversation by listing dozens of meaningful activities and ideas, like play and work, food and sleep, family and friends, security and adventure. We observed how much our fears can interfere and how courage makes the difference by overcoming the barriers and finding meaning despite them. From there, we forgot our meaning of life research project and shared stories of our favorite life experiences.

Annetta had a way of asking questions and following up with more questions that not only made me feel interesting, but brought out a depth that I wasn't accustomed to even thinking about. I could analyze other things just fine, but I had never turned such an analytical eye on myself.

Not only that, but Annetta had a way of identifying the best parts of me and shining her light on them. She was like a magnet, finding treasure hidden beneath the sand and lifting it to the surface.

I wondered if she had this effect on everyone, and whether the change was only mine – if she was a catalyst, inducing rapid change all around her but experiencing none of the same for herself.

When her turn to answer questions came, she needed no follow-up prompts. She told stories filled with vivid detail and insightful observations about life. Furthermore, her family had lived all over the world, and that supplied a wealth of experience and stories.

"That's so great," I said, "that you've been so many places. Do people who haven't traveled so much ever seem boring to you?"

"No!" she said emphatically. "Of course not. People can be so interesting for so many reasons. The most important thing — maybe the only important thing — is what they are, or who they are, on the inside. I mean, a lot of people travel all over, but they never let it get inside them, so it doesn't have any impact on them at all. What's the use of that?"

"What impact does it have on you?" I asked. "What impact should it have?"

Annetta thought for a moment. "Well, I don't know exactly. I think it has something to do with realizing what's out there. Yeah, I think that's it. It makes you realize that people are basically the same everywhere, that there's more than one good way to see the world, and more than one good way to live your life, and whatever way you choose isn't necessarily right or wrong. Maybe that makes you appreciate differences more. Or maybe it just makes you appreciate what you've got more, because it no longer seems ordinary. Or maybe..." she paused again momentarily, "I think for me, it just gave me a feeling that there are no real boundaries in life. Or any limitations, ya know? Like I can go anywhere and do anything I want. Does that make sense?"

"Yeah," I answered, "it makes lots of sense." It sounded so exciting, especially watching the way Annetta told it, and seeing the obvious passion for life flash in her eyes. "What else makes people interesting; you know, on the inside?"

"Gosh, just about any experience could do that, I think. Anything that stretches you, maybe, or, well, anything. And it probably depends a lot on who you are to begin with, way deep inside. And then on the way you're brought up, too, of course."

Annetta stopped and looked me in the eye. "That's a big question," she said.

"Just finish answering this one," I begged. "You can ask me a big one next." On some level, I realized that I was prodding Annetta because I hoped she would mention some trait that I had. I wanted some small reassurance that I had something to offer to this friendship, that she might be willing to spend more time together and not grow tired of me.

"Okay," she assented. "Anyway, this is fun to talk about." Annetta took a deep, quick breath, preparing for her last exam question. "All right. What makes people interesting." She thought for a second and then began. "This question is both hard and easy. I love when someone is aware of beauty. When they see it and it just fills them, and they think they can't express it, but if you really see into them, you know exactly how they feel. That's easy because my best friend at school was like that. He stopped trying to explain it to people, because he'd get so frustrated when they couldn't understand or appreciate it.

"I also love when people are kind. Not the cheesy, sweet, superficial way, though; not when they say all the right things just because they're trying to please everyone. But when someone really cares deep down inside, they don't even have to say anything, and you feel it, and you understand. That's easy because my dad's like that.

"And I love when people are adventurous and brave. I love when they do whatever they want and say whatever they think and just dive into life because they love it so much and they're not afraid of the consequences. My little sister Amy's so much that way that it scares me.

"And some people think they're that way, but they really do what they want because they're selfish or afraid or...I don't know what. They don't do things because they love life, but because they're avoiding discomfort, and you can tell because they're wasting their lives – wasting time, doing drugs, hurting themselves and other people.

"That's the easy part of the question. The hard part is that there are so many other things I admire so much, but I can't think of them off the top of my head. Is that good enough?"

"Absolutely."

Listening to Annetta made me feel like someone had found the dial to turn up the amount of color in the world. Every sentence opened half a dozen ideas that I wanted to follow to their ends. I watched her features – her hair, cheeks, nose and teeth, and especially the way her eyes danced when she spoke. There seemed to be an energy pulsing around the edges of her green irises.

"What's your favorite place you've ever lived?" I asked, forgetting my promise to let her ask the next question. Annetta had already listed all the places around the world her family had lived while growing up – England, Brazil, Hawaii, and various cities and towns spread throughout the U.S. Her father loved discovering new places and meeting people, and he used his career as a geologist to work alternately as a teacher or research specialist for oil and gas companies, which gave plenty of opportunity for travel.

"That's hard to say," she answered. "Partly because I was so young when we went half those places. Like in Brazil, I was seven, so I only remember my neighborhood and the American School and a few other images from the markets and places we went often.

"I remember they had stores that only sold bananas, or only bread or only something else." Annetta's eyes began to light up again as the images played through her mind. No matter how little she claimed to remember, the details in those memories remained vivid.

Everything she said – even the mundane details – seemed interesting and important. I couldn't figure out why, so I kept listening and enjoying the way her sentences filled the space between us.

"And we'd always make mom buy silver bananas, we thought they were so cool. And the people were so nice, they'd always smile at us and talk to us, but of course I had no idea what they were saying. I'm sure it was nice. It must have been strange to see a couple blonde little American kids there. And I was so shy, I'd never talk to them or hardly even look at them. Except for the guy who worked at the candy store by the church half a block from our home. We'd take our allowance there and he'd always say, 'One, two, tree! One, two, tree!' We got used to it and we'd say, "Um, dos, tres" back to him. Once his son, who must have been about twelve, walked down the street and started swearing at us in English. His father ran outside and started beating him. I felt bad for

Courage, Love and the Meaning of Christmas

him then.

"And then…," Annetta's sentence trailed off and a distant look came into her eyes. A moment later, she looked up again and said, "I talk too much."

"Not at all!" I assured her, eager for her to continue. But her mood had changed, the conversation had lost its momentum, and I didn't know how to bring it back.

"Intermission's over," Annetta said, standing up. "And Amy's big part is coming up. We'd better get back to our seats."

I stood up and obediently followed her back to the auditorium. The play had already resumed, so I sat down next to Annetta in the back of the dark auditorium and wondered what Annetta wasn't telling me, and how I could find out, and what would happen next.

16 Wishes

Amy was a senior and played Chava, the youngest of Tevye's three older daughters, and as far as we were concerned, she stole the show. She seemed to have the same energy and confidence as Annetta, but with a careless impulsiveness tossed in. When Tevye sang about losing her — my favorite part of the play — Amy danced in the background so gracefully that I actually teared up.

"Were you like that in high school?" I whispered.

"No," Annetta whispered back. "I was too shy."

The play ended and the audience gave the cast a standing ovation. We milled around for a while afterward while I was introduced to what felt like half the town.

Nearly everyone gave me a strange look that I couldn't quite interpret as we shook hands. It looked like a knowing smile, only I didn't know whatever it was they knew. After five or six people had given me the exact same look, I had a difficult time keeping myself from laughing. Annetta caught on, too, and soon we couldn't help but laugh with nearly every introduction. No one seemed to mind.

"What is that look about?" I asked when we had a moment alone.

"I think they're checking you out to decide if they approve."

"Watching out for you, eh? They must think very highly of you."

"Something like that. People can be kind of nosy around here."

The cast stood in the lobby, shaking hands with the audience as they left, and once the crowds thinned, Amy walked toward us.

"So you're Spencer, huh?" She asked, holding out her hand. "Netta told me about you."

"You were awesome up there," I told her, shaking her hand and nodding toward the stage. She still wore her costume and thick stage makeup but made it look good.

"You were right, Netta," she observed. "He *is* cute."

Annetta's jaw dropped in astonishment at her sister's boldness. "I never said that," she protested.

Amy just laughed. "You certainly implied it," she countered.

"Well," Annetta said, turning toward me, "you *are* very handsome."

"Thanks," I answered, feeling suddenly awkward.

"So, Spence," Amy began again, "how do you like my big sister?"

"Stop trying to embarrass him, Amy," Annetta cut in. Amy looked at her with a mischievous grin to see if she would really be in trouble if she didn't stop teasing. Annetta's face revealed no sign either way.

"She's pretty great," I answered anyway.

"Yep," Amy said. "You got that right. I'd better leave you two lovebirds alone now before I say something my sister will regret. Nice to meet you, Spencer."

"You, too," I answered. Amy curtsied and danced away to rejoin the other cast members.

Annetta and I pulled on our coats and made our way outside, where the night had grown cold enough to make our breath stand out as white vapor. As we crossed the bridge on the way back to my car, Annetta stopped and leaned over the concrete railing. I stopped next to her and looked down into the black river. The nearly-full moon reflected in the water, shimmering on rippled currents, dimming along the edges where the stream turned to ice.

"What is it about lights," Annetta wondered out loud, "that draws us in like moths?"

I reached into my pocket and pulled out a couple of coins. "Want to make a wish?" I asked.

Annetta took a dime from my hand and asked, "Who do you usually wish for — yourself or other people?"

"I hadn't thought about it much," I admitted, knowing that it had never occurred to me to make a wish for someone else. "What about you?"

"I always wish for other people. It's more fun that way. You can get more creative."

Annetta turned around and thought for a moment, then flipped the

Courage, Love and the Meaning of Christmas

dime over her shoulder and waited to hear it plop into the stream.

I turned around and thought for a moment, trying to think of something to wish for someone else, but couldn't think of anything more important than wishing that Annetta and I would become friends, and that I would learn how to be more audacious and live a more meaningful life. I closed my eyes, flipped my coin into the river, and made another selfish wish.

"I'm glad I met you, Spencer," Annetta said, cocking her head to one side.

"Me, too," I agreed, wondering why she said that. For split second, a crazy thought crossed my mind. *Does she like me?*

"I hadn't realized how restless I was feeling," Annetta explained, "with so few people to really talk to around here."

That makes more sense, I thought. *I'm just someone to talk to.* Anyway, she had done most of the talking. How could she like me if I hadn't even said that much?

"So thanks for asking me out," Annetta finished, looking up at me gratefully.

I smiled and looked into her eyes, and suddenly it dawned on me: she doesn't see me. She doesn't know me. She doesn't realize that she's standing here thanking a nervous, shy, insecure kid with nothing to offer but a listening ear. She sees a possible friend, a peer, maybe even a man. She thinks we have things in common. She thinks she can talk to me on her level.

But sensing Annetta see me this way had a surprising effect – I automatically began to see myself as she did. I felt stronger, smarter, and more interesting. And then I realized: *maybe she's right! Maybe there's more to me than I knew, and I have been the blind one.*

And why not?! Why not become confident and outgoing and interesting? Why not rewrite my character right now? I was tired of playing the coward! That role got me nowhere, and I was tired of being nowhere! I would practice acting confidently until it became real. From now on, I would act audaciously and stop always assuming the worst.

"My pleasure," I replied, still looking Annetta in the eye and feeling the solid new feeling surge inside. "Let's do it again soon."

"Yeah," Annetta agreed, smiling happily.

A cold breeze drifted downstream and made us turn away from the river. Annetta pulled her jacket tighter around her neck and shivered, and we both turned and walked back to the car.

I unlocked the car door and let Annetta in, and we drove the five blocks to her home. I pulled up to the curb and we stayed in the car with the engine and heater running off and on for another hour, talking about people we had known, things we had done, places she had gone, and things we each hoped for in the future.

Finally, she glanced up at the clock on the dash. "I'd better go."

"I'll call you tomorrow," I promised, "and we can set up something fun."

"I don't work until four," she offered.

"How about lunch?" I proposed. "I know this great diner in town. Named 'Becca's.' Ever heard of it? I'm told everything on the menu is delish."

Annetta laughed and shook her head. "Please, no! The last thing I need is to spend ten hours at work tomorrow! Why don't I drop by your place?"

"Twelve o'clock?"

"Yeah. I'll be there."

With that, Annetta reached over and gave my hand a squeeze, then opened her door and ran inside.

17 Grandpa

I woke up late the next morning feeling utterly refreshed. I stared out the window for a while at the rolling, snow-covered hills, relishing the freedom of vacation and playing all my memories of last night over and over in my head, then finally rolled out of bed sometime after ten o'clock. I wandered downstairs in my pajamas and found a stack of cold pancakes with scrambled eggs and sausage on the side that Grandma had left in the oven for me.

"We're gonna have to get Grandma a microwave one of these days," I said out loud as I poured maple syrup over the plate and pulled a gallon of milk from the fridge. I could easily have turned on the oven to warm everything up, but I had learned to tolerate cold food to match my hectic college schedule.

Grandma walked into the kitchen as I was beginning to wash my dishes and picked up the dish cloth to dry them.

"How did your evening turn out?" she asked.

"Fantastic," I answered. "The play was really good and Annetta and I had a great conversation."

Grandma didn't say anything more, but I could tell she was happy. I

Courage, Love and the Meaning of Christmas

could tell that the matchmaker gears and wheels inside her mind were spinning.

"Tell me about how you and Grandpa met," I said. I knew that she came from a high-class family and he was a farmer, I knew they met at a boarding house where she lived while going to college, but I felt curious about her first impression of him, about their first conversation, about what attracted them to each other, and exactly how things had progressed.

"I was a coed at the University of Utah and had the world at my feet," Grandma began the familiar story. "I was a member of the most popular sorority on campus, I was dating a dashing basketball player from a wealthy family, I had a few pieces of my art displayed in a downtown gallery, and one year left until graduation.

"One day my boyfriend, who was a senior, had the audacity to suggest that I abandon my studies to marry him and move to California for his upcoming career at a prestigious law office.

"Well, naturally, I wouldn't hear of it and we had our first real argument. I certainly thought highly of myself in those days!" Grandma smiled broadly and I imagined she was thinking of her wealthy family who had spoiled her and raised her to accept only the best, and the blow they were about to receive.

"So when an awkward farm boy appeared at the dinner table that night, I made a point of directing all my attention toward him and away from my fuming boyfriend.

"Little did I know that Andrew had not appeared there by chance! He had seen me walk down the sidewalk while running some errands in town and somehow made up his mind that we would meet and marry."

Grandma paused for a moment to smile before continuing. "So when he noticed some broken planks on the picket fence of my boarding house, he strode up to the front door, told my landlady that she had such a beautiful house and it was a shame to see the broken planks and would she mind if he fixed them for her?

"His plan was to work slowly enough to catch me as I walked by, though I'm certain he had no idea what he would say to me. What luck when my landlady invited him to dinner! My poor father!" she exclaimed then. "I don't think he ever understood how I could abandon my studies to marry a farm boy!"

Now Grandma laughed out loud. Apparently she still retained some of her old stubborn independence and enjoyed reliving the memory.

She looked at me then, put down the dish she had been drying for the last two minutes, and gave me a strong hug. "And now I have an entire wonderful family to show for it!" she exclaimed.

I hugged her back, then asked, "What was it about Grandpa that brought you together?"

"He was so real," Grandma answered without hesitation. "He was genuine and direct, and when I noticed how angry and confused my many suitors became when they saw me spending time with a country bumpkin, I intentionally spent more and more time with him, for the sheer pleasure of watching them fume. I was such a tart, wasn't I?" she added with a smile.

"And the angrier they grew, and the more they ruffled their feathers and tried to impress me with their money and titles and prestige, the more I grew tired of their company. Eventually, it dawned on me that I liked myself better with Andrew, that I loved him, and when he proposed and asked me to return to Wyoming with him, I couldn't refuse."

"Did you know what you were getting yourself into?" I asked.

"Oh, not in the least!" Grandma assured me. "I never dreamt that I would be expected to wake up early and do farm work – in my daydreams, servants would do all the chores and I would simply play the beautiful country princess." Grandma chuckled again at the memory.

"The first day after our honeymoon, Andrew took me out to the barn and showed me how to milk a cow. I thought it was interesting and kind of him to show me around. When he suggested I give it a try, I told him no thanks. The perplexed expression on his face was precious! No less so, I'm certain, than the consternation and shock on mine when he explained that I would be milking the cows from then on!

"I stomped out of the barn in such a huff that I splashed cow manure all over my ankles. When I complained that the conditions in the barn were too untidy for me to ever possibly work there, Andrew assigned me another task – cleaning the barn.

"I tried everything to get out of my chores, but to no avail. Andrew wouldn't budge. I spilled the milk, complained endlessly, begged, cried, feigned illness and injury, and even burned his meals.

"Andrew had no patience for such nonsense nor any sympathy for my tantrums. I wasted the better part of a year feeling short changed and upset about my lot in life before confessing that it got me nowhere to do my work so begrudgingly, and deciding that I may as well learn to

Courage, Love and the Meaning of Christmas

approach my chosen lot more optimistically.

"I stopped complaining, did my chores without needing to be woken up several times first, prepared wonderful Sunday dinners, and painted and decorated the barn more to my taste."

Here Grandma sighed contentedly. "That's when your grandfather and I truly fell in love. Beyond his simple, somewhat austere exterior, his heart could hold so much love. When I learned to see that…" Grandma trailed off, shaking her head and smiling softly. "We didn't always agree, but we never quarreled again."

On one hand, Grandma's story sounded happy and perfect and miraculous, like they were meant to end up together and heaven had interfered to make sure they did. On the other hand, the match seemed awkward and unlikely and difficult. I liked hearing Grandma tell it, but didn't know exactly what to think of it all.

18 Eyes

Annetta showed up a few minutes early for lunch. We ate venison sandwiches and I was surprised at how well Grandma and Annetta seemed to know each other.

After lunch, Grandma excused herself, citing some errand she needed to run in town.

"Where were we?" I asked as Annetta and I sat across the table from each other.

"I think we're still somewhere in the middle," Annetta answered.

"Ah, yes," I said, "the middle." I felt the panic begin to rise in my throat as I sought frantically for something to say before the silence grew uncomfortable.

"Also," Annetta added, "I did most of the talking last night, so it's your turn."

"Oh, good," I said nervously. "Let's see," I continued, scanning my brain for a conversation topic. "The middle. Where to begin? There's so much to choose from."

"Pick a number," Annetta said.

"Six," I answered, wondering what the number was for.

"Okay, start at six."

What? I wondered, and then I got it. Six years old. That narrowed things down considerably. At six, I went to first grade, rarely spoke up in class, had only one best friend, and spent the summer here in

Amber.

"Do you want to go for a walk?" I blurted out.

"Sure," Annetta said after a short pause.

We put on our coats and began walking up the road, away from Amber and toward the rolling hills. "I used to spend summers here as a kid," I began, and surprised myself with how much I had to say about it. I described the places I played as we walked by them, the imaginary adventures, my loving grandparents, and the pure happiness that I felt only here. Annetta helped by asking lots of questions to make me look deeper into my memories and thoughts, and by sharing her own stories about growing up.

The air was a balmy 40 degrees and the sun shone beautifully on the snow-covered ground. We walked for almost an hour before running out of things to say. This time, however, I didn't panic. I had grown more comfortable with Annetta and with myself. I had grown more aware of my thoughts, memories and feelings, and more confident that they weren't boring and pointless, at least not for someone like Annetta who seemed to find them interesting. The conversation thus far had left dozens of unfinished loose ends and I no longer worried so much about running out of things to say.

We both stopped atop a rise in the road and took in the view of the Amber Valley. A cloud shadow passed over us and without the sun, the breeze suddenly felt cold. "That's all I've got for six," I said. "Shall we turn around?"

The way back was filled with both conversation and silence, enjoying the fresh air and each other's company even without words.

At home, we sat on the living room couch. Annetta sat sideways with one leg crossed under the other, facing me. I had run out of stories to tell and thoughts to share, but this time the silence didn't feel uncomfortable. Annetta sat comfortably leaning against the couch and I noticed a soft glow in her beautiful green eyes.

"Let's trade questions," Annetta suggested.

"Okay," I agreed. "What does that mean?"

"It means we take turns asking questions. You go first."

"I just did," I said. "It's your turn."

"That didn't count!" Annetta objected. "But okay. My first question is…." She paused and looked me in the eye for a moment before continuing. "What do you like best about yourself?"

I thought for a second, but nothing came to mind. "I thought you weren't supposed to say good things about yourself," I said, avoiding the question.

"Why not?" Annetta demanded.

"Just so you don't sound vain or proud, I guess."

Annetta's expression changed subtly. Some of the light left her eyes. She suddenly seemed to be seeing me from a distance, as if something had just reminded her that I was a stranger and we had known each other for less than a day. As if the real me had just shown through my façade of confidence or the illusion she had created for me from the beginning.

"But that's dumb, isn't it?" I tried. Annetta's expression didn't change, but she seemed to be waiting for me to continue. "Why should I care what anyone thinks?" Annetta's mouth showed a hint of a smile again and she nodded her head slightly. I had found the right thing to say to perpetuate the illusion. Annetta continued to wait patiently. "All right then," I continued, "we'll make our own rules."

"Better rules," Annetta added.

"Yeah," I agreed, "better because...."

"Because we do what's best for us," she interrupted.

"And it makes more sense to recognize what's good about ourselves rather than pretend to be humble so no one calls us vain and become less than we are." *Of course!* I thought. *That's how I became so shy in the first place, by focusing on my weaknesses all the time. Maybe I can turn it all around by changing my point of view.*

"Okay, then. What I like best about myself is...." I paused again. I honestly couldn't think of anything to say. I knew what I liked to do, I knew my favorite food was pizza and my favorite color was blue, but I didn't have a clue as to what I liked best about myself.

"Isn't it funny," Annetta asked, "how hard it can be to buck the norm and stand up for yourself?"

"An example of when courage makes a difference, right?"

"Exactly," Annetta agreed. She must have seen that I was honestly stuck. "Want some help?"

"Yeah," I answered, "sure."

"All right," she offered. "I'll tell you what I like best about you, and you can answer later."

I felt a little uncomfortable At first, as she looked steadily into my eyes. I felt like she was looking right through me. I could almost feel her prying through my thoughts and memories, and I wondered what she would find there.

Then I noticed her eyes again. At first,, I focused only on the bright green color that glowed in the early afternoon light shining through the windows, but soon the other glow, the deeper light that shone from somewhere deep inside her soul, captured my attention.

In it I saw, or rather felt, all the things she had told me about last night – her love of beauty, of people and travel, of life and experience. I sensed a mixture of compassion and sternness, a willingness to give openly, but an unwillingness to let anyone take what they didn't have the right to. I felt a deep yearning for connection and love, but something stood in the way of it all, guarding it and preventing anyone from entering there.

I didn't fully understand all this right then, I couldn't have put it into words yet, but sensing all this suddenly made me feel more complete than I ever had before. As if I had found something to lean against and rest from all my worries and fears. As if all my old insecurities could drown in her eyes and never return. As if I finally found a secure path to follow where I could start walking and never look back. As if I had been waiting all this time, waiting to know the end of the path before I would commit myself to it, but suddenly the unknown didn't seem so daunting or dangerous; as if I had lost my fear of the dark.

I was so lost in my thoughts and feelings that she startled me when she began to speak.

"You're one of the most interesting people I've ever met," she said, sounding surprised and curious. "You have so much potential that you haven't even discovered. So much wisdom and passion and intensity and love and strength just waiting to be unleashed.

"But…you're waiting for something. Waiting for the right time to begin or for direction or to know the end of the road before you'll start walking. Like you think you're confused, when really you simply don't know everything yet and expect to have all the answers from the outset."

How could she know that?!

"You have such capacity for joy," she continued, "but you don't know that either. You think life is hard. They go hand in hand, you know, joy and pain? The suffering carves you out and makes room for the joy."

Annetta paused again, still looking into my eyes, then shook her head. "There's more, but I don't understand it yet."

"What do you mean?" I asked. "How do you do that?"

"I don't know how it works," she explained. "My dad taught us how to do it when we were little. You just look someone in the eye and clear your mind, then you start feeling what the other person is like. It's like seeing with different eyes or sensing them through some invisible connection between people. He says most people do it without ever noticing. Haven't you ever looked at someone and felt like you knew all about them, or heard about twins who always know when the other one is in trouble?"

I remembered what I had just sensed in her eyes and nodded my head. "So what about you?" I asked, eager to find out more about this surprising girl. "What do you like best about yourself?"

"I don't know, either," she confessed, smiling wryly. "I just like being alive."

I looked steadily into her eyes, getting ready to take my turn and tell her what I liked best about her, but I couldn't see anything beyond the rich green of her irises. Her steady gaze sat perfectly framed by her oval face and gentle features. Her mouth looked small until she smiled, her lips looked soft and inviting…and the thought of kissing them tied my stomach into a knot. All my insecurities jumped to the foreground and I found myself tongue tied and speechless.

I tried to imagine us together. I tried to imagine how it would feel to reach out and take her hand. I imagined leaning forward and wrapping my arms around her shoulders and waist and pulling her body tight against me. I struggled against the fears and nervousness and panic that the mere thought sent surging in my throat.

I suddenly grew aware again of Annetta's return gaze as she watched me curiously for a moment. My anxiety turned up a notch as I wondered if she was reading my mind again, but then the grandfather clock in the corner chimed 3:30 and Annetta looked away. "I'd better go."

I followed her out to her car and she turned and wrapped her arms around my neck for a quick hug. I held her close and didn't let go when she relaxed her embrace. She gave me another squeeze, a little longer this time, then relaxed again and I let her go.

"Call me," she said with a happy smile, then got in her car and drove away.

19 Amber, Wyoming

After another late, cold breakfast the next morning, I wandered outside to find something to do. The cool air felt refreshing and woke me up like a gentle slap in the face. With a few inches of snow on the ground, there wasn't any yard work to do, so I walked to the barn to chop more wood. As I swung the door open, my eyes fell on Grandpa's truck. The old four-wheel drive had been used for years to haul firewood and the family Christmas tree down from the hills. Now his snowmobile sat in the bed, where it had probably rested since last Christmas vacation when I took it out for a ride with my little sisters.

I opened the driver's door and slid onto the vinyl seat. The key still dangled from the ignition, and I reached out and turned it, wondering if the battery would still work. Sure enough, the engine turned over two or three times and then started, running fast with the choke wide open. I wanted to take it out for a spin, maybe drive blind through the dry corn stalks just for fun, but bouncing around in the field wouldn't be a good idea with the snowmobile in the back.

It also wouldn't be a very good idea, I realized, to fill the barn with exhaust fumes if I planned to work in here, so I shut off the engine and climbed out of the cab. I chopped enough wood to heat the house for a week or two, then found a few things to straighten up in the back of the barn. Finally I went back inside to shower and decide what to do with my day.

I wished I had brought some books with me, but when I left school right after finals, reading was the last thing I wanted to do over the break. Now I could read for pleasure and that would be different. I regretted my lack of foresight, but I could always stop by the library later.

I wandered around the house for a while, looking into the rooms and out the windows. I made a few trips to the barn and stocked the wood bins next to the wood burning stoves on each of the three floors of the house. I washed the breakfast dishes and began to pace the house. I usually enjoy solitude, but all this silence started making me restless. "We've got to get Grandma an internet connection one of these days," I thought out loud.

Just when I was ready to jump in my car to drive into town and have lunch at the café — not a bad idea, I thought — Grandma pulled up out front and I walked outside to meet her.

"Hey Grandma, what do you usually do around here all day?" I asked.

"Oh, I don't spend much time here," she said. "Will you help me carry these bags inside?"

I opened the back door of her car and picked up four bags of groceries. This was only the beginning of what we would use to feed our extended family in the coming week or two. Grandma held the door for me and I carried everything to the kitchen counter where we began putting it away.

"So what do you do with yourself?" I asked, piling cans of yams and evaporated milk into the cupboard.

"Oh, I have some friends. Sometimes we quilt or knit for our grandchildren, and we did some gardening and painting over the summer. Sometimes we just visit. And everyone knows who to call when the community needs anything."

"That's great, Grandma," I said. "It sounds like everything's going pretty well for you here."

"Yes, I've no room to complain," she answered. "But it certainly is nice to come home and find someone here to greet me."

"Well, you know this house has always been one of my favorite places."

We finished with the groceries and Grandma set out some home-baked rolls and fixings for sandwiches. I set to slicing a tomato. "How long has Annetta's family lived here?" I asked.

"Not long," Grandma answered. "Only about six years."

I guess that wasn't long in a small community like this where many families ran back for generations. And about six years ago was when I had gotten my driver's license and gotten too busy playing or working minimum-wage jobs to spend entire summers here. I felt a slight twinge of regret that it had cost me the chance to meet Annetta that much sooner.

"I'm going to town with a few friends to do some Christmas shopping — if we buy anything here, everyone knows what they're getting long before Christmas arrives. If you wouldn't mind driving me in to town to meet my friends, maybe you could run into Annetta there. I could call and tell everyone to meet at Becca's."

Sometimes "town" meant Amber, five miles away. Sometimes it meant Evanston, another eighty miles down the road. Eventually, you learned to tell them apart by context or a slight change in inflection. "Sure, Grandma. I was meaning to go into town myself anyway." I wondered if I had put the right inflection on "town".

We finished lunch and drove to the diner. I looked inside through the window but only saw the boy from last night behind the counter. Two of Grandma's friends were waiting in the parking lot, discussing whose car they should drive.

"Eleanor's not here yet," Grandma said. "Spencer, would you go inside and call to see if she's coming?"

I almost asked why they didn't just text her, but immediately remembered that there was no cell service in Amber Valley. I had turned off my useless phone and packed it away the morning after I arrived.

"Eleanor's always late," said one friend. "Don't worry about her."

"Why don't you go in and see if she's on her way," Grandma persisted. Her friend was about to argue, but Grandma gave her a look that she must have understood.

"Well, go check, then!" she said. "You heard what Sophie said."

I walked inside and up the to the bar.

"Netta ain't here," said the boy.

"I'm not looking for her," I answered. "Do you have a phone around here?"

"There's a pay phone in front of the truck stop."

"Jim!" a voice shouted from back in the kitchen. "Don't be such a jerk!" Amy stepped out and up to the counter. "You can use this one," she said, pulling a phone out from below the counter and setting it in front of me. "Jimmy," she added, pointing a finger up at the tall, skinny boy. "Behave!" She added a little punch to his shoulder and walked back to the kitchen.

I picked up the receiver. "Would you ring Eleanor for me, please?" I said. Half the town still ran on a party line. Just like in the early days of telephone, people would sometimes listen in on other's conversations just for fun. With modern technology, you could even turn on your speakerphone and hit mute and listen to every call without anyone hearing you breathing on the line. News traveled fast.

"Eleanor's gone to town to do some Christmas shopping," the operator told me.

"Do you know if she's left yet?"

"Probably not yet. She's always a little late. Shall I ring her line?"

"No, that's all right. Thanks a lot."

"You're welcome. Who is this, anyway?"

I almost had to laugh. I had never experienced this level of service from the phone company before. "Spencer Cook," I answered.

"Ah, yes, I remember. I met you the other night after the play. Parlez-vous français?"

"Uh, no."

"Ah, well. Netta doesn't work till six."

"Oh? Well, uh, thanks."

Courage, Love and the Meaning of Christmas

"I just thought since you were at Becca's, you might have been looking for her."

I suddenly remembered the face that belonged to the voice on the other end of the line. It was a small woman who had introduced herself to us at the school play, asked lots of questions, and had seemed to know the latest gossip about everyone. Now I knew why. "All right, well, I'll catch up with her somewhere else."

"She lives in the white house at the end of Juniper Drive."

"Thanks. I'll try her there."

"Oh, good," she said slowly, and then I understood why Annetta had answered all her questions with brief and vague generalities last night. Oh, well, so what if the word gets out that I like her? I didn't see how that could do me any harm.

"Oh, by the way, do you know what time the library closes?" I asked.

"Five o'clock," she answered. "What kinds of books do you like to read?"

"Oh, I just thought I'd go see what caught my eye. Thanks for everything. Bye."

I hung up the phone as the woman struggled to find another question to keep me on the line. When I walked back outside, the women were still discussing whose car to take, and the choice seemed to be leaning toward the woman who had spoken to me before. They looked up as I walked out. "Looks like she'll be a bit late," I said, and they all nodded.

Amy followed me outside just then. "Hey, Spence," she said. "C'mon back in here and have a lemonade with me." She stood there in her white t-shirt and apron, folding her arms against her body and gripping her arms tightly for protection against the cold air. "You're not in a hurry are ya?"

"No, not at all."

"Then c'mon. And don't mind Jim, he's just jealous."

I said goodbye to Grandma and her friends and followed Amy back inside, where she led me to a table with two lemonades already waiting. I sat down and picked up the glass nearest me. The glass was warm, almost hot.

"Warm lemonade?" I asked.

"Try it," she said, picking up her own glass and sipping.

I put the glass to my lips and sipped. It was sweeter and smoother than usual, and very good.

"I put some honey in it," Amy said. "Good, huh?"

"Yeah, it's great," I answered, taking another sip.

"I thought you'd like it, being such a big fan of lemonade," she said.

"Oh, well, I'm not really that big of a fan — until now, I mean, this is great — but yesterday was just...well, it's a long story."

"So tell me," Amy said. "You're not in any hurry, are ya? And I promise not to spread it through the whole town like Andrea."

"The operator?" I asked, taking another swallow.

"You guessed it. I heard her grilling you. I thought you handled her very expertly — especially the way you hung up without being rude — that's tough!" Amy laughed out loud. "But don't mind my eavesdropping. You know a dozen other people were pricking up their ears all over town to get the latest action. When you think about it, it's kinda like a primitive version of Facebook."

"Oh, I don't mind. I think it's funny."

"So tell me your lemonade story," Amy commanded.

"There's not much to tell. I was just having a conversation with a friend before I left school about what it means to be great, and he said that if you just do what you feel like, then that's how you be great."

Amy just stared at me for a moment. "Sounds kind of selfish to me," she said.

"Yeah, well, Ski has his own ways of doing things."

"His name is Ski?"

"Yeah. Well, that's his middle name, but he goes by it."

"So what does doing what you feel like have to do with lemonade?"

"Oh, he was just saying how he'd like to go drink some lemonade on the beach, so...."

"And he thinks drinking lemonade on the beach would make him great? Are you sure he wasn't planning to mix in a little alcohol to add to his delusions of grandeur?"

"Oh, no, it's just that, well, he was just making the point that he's not out to impress anybody else, that's all."

"I guess that part could be good," Amy admitted, pursing her pink lips and nodding. "So what do you think?"

"I haven't made up my mind quite," I confessed. "But Annetta said something the other night that I liked a lot — that courage is what makes the difference or something like that."

"Oh, yeah. 'Courage changes everything.' She wrote that in a letter home from school once and now our dad says it all the time." Amy rolled her eyes like she was tired of hearing it. "Listen, Spen, I better get back to work, but I've decided I like you. And so does Netta, even though she won't admit it to anyone yet. Don't go by the house till after five, 'cause dad will want to meet you before you take Netta out again. She'd want you to come by right away, but it'll be best if you wait. Oh, and call her Netta. Nobody calls her Annetta, and it sounds so formal. And don't tell her I told you all this or she'll kill me."

"Thanks, Am," I said. "You're a real sweetheart."

"Yep. Treat my sister right and I'll stay that way." She winked but her expression was serious. "And one more thing — everybody goes snowmobiling on Saturdays. You're coming tomorrow, okay?"

"Yeah, sure, I'd love to."

Amy picked up our empty glasses and disappeared into the kitchen. I said bye to Jim on the way out. Grandma and her friends had already left for town and left me wondering how to kill four and a half hours until five o'clock.

20 Q & A

I got in my car and drove over to the library. The old hardwood floors squeaked lightly as I walked in, but not loudly enough to wake the librarian dozing behind the reference desk. He looked comfortable and I was glad to have the place to myself. I wandered the aisles, scanning book titles and hoping something would catch my attention.

The floor squeaked again near the reference desk and I assumed the librarian had woken up. I'd just keep quiet and he'd never know I was here.

The books didn't always seem to follow any particular order. It seemed like some shelves had simply been arranged as the books arrived. In a section mixed with classics, science fiction, and history, I found a copy of *Les Miserables* and pulled it from the shelf. I had always wanted to read it, but had never gotten around to it.

I felt a light tap on my shoulder and spun around, startled. There stood Annetta grinning up at me. "Hi," she whispered. Her green eyes sparkled and she looked happy to see me. "I saw your car out front."

"You look great," I said and surprised myself by not tensing up.

"Whatcha reading?" she asked.

"I was looking for anything good," I answered. "Got any recommendations?"

"That's a good one," she said, pulling the book from my fingers. "One of the best, in fact." Just then the entrance floorboards squeaked again. Annetta grabbed my arm and tugged me down the aisle. "This way, quick!" she said. We ran as quietly as possible to a back corner of the library and she opened a small door leading into a room with a few chairs, a large wooden table, and walls full of dusty books. "This is where I always come when I don't want to be disturbed or spied on." She closed the door silently and we sat down at the table.

"Yesterday was fun," I said, eager to start up where we left off.

She nodded her head in agreement, then launched directly into a continuation of our interrupted conversation. "You still owe me some answers."

"Then you owe me some questions."

Annetta shook her head at that. "As I recall, I asked you a question," she reminded me, "and somehow ended up answering it, too."

"I'll answer this time," I promised.

"Okay," she assented. "What attribute do you most want to develop?"

"Courage," I answered quickly.

"Three points for speed," she said with a half smile, "and minus five for insincerity. Your turn."

I didn't have such good questions at the tip of my tongue. I'd have to make up the difference with more speed points. When nothing came to mind quickly, I fell back on a time-proven classic.

"What's your favorite color?" I asked.

"Blue. No, green. Or red. Or yellow!" she appended at the last second, then confessed, "I don't really have favorites. I just like everything. What good is having a favorite if it limits you to only one choice?"

Wow. Maybe there was no such thing as a simple, ordinary question with this girl. Before I had a chance to ponder the implications of her answer, she came at me with her next question.

"What is the hardest thing you've ever done?"

It's no wonder Netta ended up doing most of the talking. I didn't have quick answers for any of her questions, but she never ran out of things to say. So rather than thinking and figuring everything out this time, I just said the first thing that came to my mind. "Just living."

"Elaborate," she commanded.

"Growing up," I continued. "Moving along day by day when you never have time to figure out exactly where you're heading or what you really hope for. Just meeting all the day-to-day challenges means you never quite catch up with yourself."

"Give me a concrete example," she demanded.

Courage, Love and the Meaning of Christmas

"Well," I thought, "that's hard, because after all the little trials pass, then they don't matter anymore and you see that they weren't such a big deal in the first place, but that's hindsight and it doesn't make the present moment any easier."

"Good answer," Annetta said, "but give me a specific example of one of the little trials."

"I think it's now my turn to ask a question," I objected.

"Then ask."

"What's your greatest goal?"

"Just to live," Annetta answered quickly, then moved immediately back to her question. "Give me an example."

"Elaborate," I told her.

"Too slow," she ruled. "I already asked my question."

I got the impression that once she had her mind made up, arguing would do no good. "Okay. Waking up in the morning when you know you just have to work all day and you still won't catch up. Things like that."

Netta thought about that for a moment, then nodded her head. "Good enough. Your turn."

Every now and then I felt an impulse to glance at my phone, to check my messages and make sure I wasn't missing out on anything interesting. My follow-up thought each time was how grateful I felt for the lack of service in Amber and for Annetta's undivided attention as a result. Anywhere else in the world, dozens of guys would be constantly clamoring for the attention of a pretty, intelligent, charming girl like this.

We swapped questions for another half hour, sometimes laughing, sometimes following ideas and tangents, sometimes asking pointless questions just to keep the momentum going.

"What's the square root of two thousand six hundred and four?"

Annetta paused and gave me a withering look that said *are you serious?* "I don't know," she answered. "Fifty something. What's your greatest fear?"

A few days ago, I'd have known the answer: talking to Julie and revealing the fool I was. Somehow I had gotten through that one and things had turned out – not great, but far better than I had feared.

And now? Maybe fear of reverting to my cowardly self and wasting my life and never getting what I really want. And what did I really want? I was beginning to suspect that it was Annetta. So I didn't dare admit to my greatest fear, because then she would ask a follow up question and I wasn't ready to tell her that I wanted her. I would have to build up my courage for a while first.

"Me?" I asked innocently. "Afraid?"

"Answering with another question is not allowed. What's your greatest fear?"

"Giant, ravenous, super-intelligent, man-eating bats."

Annetta laughed so hard at the unexpected answer that tears came to her eyes. "Liar!" she accused.

"What's your biggest fear?" I shot back at her.

"Clowns."

"Liar," I accused back.

"Giant clowns who knock down sky scrapers and shoot acid from their eyes."

I just shook my head incredulously.

"Do I have to be honest?" she asked.

"Of course. What good is asking and answering questions if you're not honest?"

She lowered her eyes and thought for a moment longer. "Then I pass on that question," she finally said.

"Not fair," I objected again. "What good is asking questions if you don't answer them?"

Annetta ended the argument by refusing to argue. She reached across the table and held one of my hands, then begged with a shy smile, "Ask me a different question?"

I squeezed her hand back and felt my heart rate double. I definitely wanted this girl! I imagined driving up from school on weekends, sometimes bringing Annetta down to school to meet my friends, take her hiking in the snow or through Spring wildflowers, and growing to be the best of friends or better.

Impulsively, I slid one hand up her wrist to wrap my fingers around her elbow and draw her a little closer to me, then without thinking, asked the first question that came to mind. "Do you think you might like me as much as I think I like you?"

Annetta's smile faded. "What are you trying to do to me?" she asked slowly. Her eyebrows raised and I watched her eyes brim with gently sparkling warm water, though no tear ran down her cheek. She looked half happy, half in heaven, and half tired, like the question had hurt her.

I wanted to answer her question, but I didn't understand her reaction and had no idea what I should say. She watched me for a moment longer before looking down at the table and our hands. She let go of

Courage, Love and the Meaning of Christmas

mine and picked up the book again.

"Shall we read?" she asked. I nodded and she began to read out loud from chapter one. A few pages later, the moment had passed, leaving me to wonder what it all meant.

21 Letting Go

The early chapters of *Les Mis* follow the life of the priest Bienvenue. Because the musical could never hope to cover all the detail of the seven-hundred-page book, the play only touches on Bienvenue lightly and the depth and richness of detail that Hugo built around the man surprised me. Even knowing that the priest was a fictional character did not detract from the inspiration of his driving ambition to do good.

Sometimes I got caught up in the story and listened to the plot, ideas and details, picturing them clearly in my mind. Other times I stared at Annetta's face and listened to her clear, pretty voice as she read.

After three chapters, she closed the book. "This is my favorite part of the book," she said. "Everyone sees this musical and thinks Jean Valjean is the hero, and of course he is, but Bienvenue's the one I admire most."

"Why's that?" I asked.

"Well, the good thing about Valjean is that he changes dramatically and becomes so good and he's so giving. Bienvenue was never uneducated or a criminal, so he can't change that same way, but he does everything he can to have the best influence possible on the world. He's ambitious, but his goal is still selfless. I also like that even when he thinks he's been doing everything right, he's still humble enough to learn to be better. I think someone should write another entire musical just about him."

Annetta seemed entirely herself again, and whatever had affected her in our earlier conversation had vanished completely.

"And the one thing I don't like so much about Valjean is that he totally sacrifices everything for Cosette and Marius in the end. It's the martyr thing. Everyone treats it like such an admirable act, but the fact is, if he'd have been a little more selfish and taken care of his own needs, too, and asked for what he needed, asked not to be left all alone, then everyone would have been happier and suffered less and been better off.

"Anyway, I know this was a good ending for the book, because it was written to make a statement about society back then, and maybe now, too, but...but I'd just rather be more like Bienvenue than Valjean, and it makes me sad when I see people suffering when it doesn't do anyone any good."

Netta stopped then and looked up. "Oh!" she gasped. "I'm sorry, you haven't read it yet! I'm so sorry!"

"That's okay," I assured her. "I've heard the music, so I know the basic story line."

Netta dropped her head again here. "Did you know," she asked without looking up, "that your grandmother is like that?"

"Like what?" I asked. "What do you mean?"

"I mean that she's been terribly lonely since her husband died."

The only times I had seen Grandma since then were with the whole family gathered together, and she seemed anything but lonely then. The images of seeing her look so tired when she walked in the house yesterday, and the tears in her eyes when she told me how happy she was that I had come to visit early flashed through my mind. "How do you know?" I asked.

"I just know," she answered. "She stays busy and hides it really well. I think she does this because she doesn't want to burden anyone else, and she frankly doesn't believe there's anything anyone could do to help anyway.

"Most people are happy to ignore it because they're busy hiding their own pain. It's kind of an unspoken pact. Everyone just wants to avoid the pain of bringing up old wounds, and they get by pretty well for the most part, but when the wounds are fresh and deep, you know, they just won't heal without a little air, without a little love." Annetta's brow furrowed lightly as she spoke.

"I visit her sometimes," she continued. "I find little excuses to drop in, or sometimes I just knock on the door when I know she's there and we talk. She really is one of the best people in town. Sometimes I think this community would just fall apart if she left. I wish I could have met her husband, too, but I hardly spent any time in Amber until this summer, always working and going to school, ya know, and just coming for the holidays and a week or two each summer. I get the impression that those two were the models for everyone else in this town, and now Sophie is directly involved in so many people's lives and they love her, but there's really no one who can take Andrew's place."

I sighed. I didn't know what I could do to help, but I was determined to find something. I was determined to be there and to make sure Grandma had some of the love, of the air, that she needed. "I'm sure

glad you're around, Netta," I said. "I mean, I'm doubly glad you're here."
I reached up and took her hand on the table and she looked up into my
eyes. I looked down after a moment, and we both sat in silence and our
own thoughts for a while. Finally, she pulled her hand away and spoke
again.

"Listen, I have to tell you the truth — Andrea called and told me
I'd find your car here. Of course she also asked if I was coming right
over, and I said, 'Oh, I wouldn't dream of ruining all the fun you and
the network could have finding out for yourselves.' So I waited fifteen
minutes, finished up what I was doing, and went out the back door and
around the long way to avoid the main spies in town. I usually don't
care that people are watching, but if I didn't sneak a little, the library
would be swarmed by more visitors than it's had all year and we'd have
no peace and quiet."

"So how do you like living here?" I asked. "Does it ever bother you?"

Annetta thought about her answer for a moment and when she
answered, I had the impression that she hadn't said everything on
her mind. "Almost everyone's really great," she answered, pursing her
lips thoughtfully. "There are a few strange ones, but they keep life
interesting."

"What do you usually do around here? Do you ever get bored?" I
suddenly realized that I was setting up to ask her out again. I knew she
worked tonight, and tomorrow everyone was going snowmobiling—I
hoped that included Annetta.

"Yeah. Sometimes I miss school and all my friends there." She smiled
as she thought about them. "We used to skip class on a whim and
drive down the coast to Mexico. There was a little beach just before
Ensenada that we'd have all to ourselves. We used to build bonfires and
sometimes not come home till the next morning, just in time for class."

"Back when I used to come here for summers as a kid," I reminisced,
"I didn't need anything more than a little motorcycle and Grandpa or a
cousin or somebody else to play with. We used to hop on that bike and
go exploring. Now I realize we never got more than a mile or two away
from the house. Everything was simple back then, but now...now I don't
think I could stay around here for that long."

"That's what I thought when I first got up here after graduating this
summer," Annetta agreed. "I guess I still think that, but you kind of get
used to it. Maybe if I didn't know this wouldn't be forever, I'd go crazy,
but I think I'll be a little sad to leave now. You get used to things, ya
know?"

"Do you already have plans for where you'll go next?" I hoped it would be somewhere closer to Logan and school. Maybe she hadn't found a job yet and I could convince her to look somewhere close enough to drive to at least on weekends, maybe more. I hoped it wouldn't be as far as Southern California, where trips would be limited to Spring Break or other long weekends.

"Yeah," she answered, a look of concern appearing on her face. "We're moving to France next month. My dad got a teaching position in Marseilles. I assumed the gossip would have gotten around to you already. I didn't realize how I had come to depend on it."

I felt crushed inside. I didn't have any right to expect anything from Annetta, I knew, but nevertheless I had gotten my hopes up and the disappointment was hard to conceal. "Your whole family? How long will you be there?"

"Three years," Netta answered. "But I might not stay the whole time. I haven't thought it over that much."

"Promise to write?" I asked, still trying to hide my disappointment the best I could, knowing full well she would see right through me, and hoping desperately that she felt the loss, too.

"Of course I'll write, Spencer," she said, and this time it was her who took my hand in both of hers. "I hope you know how much I like you," she added. "I wasn't going to say that, to you or anyone, because I knew I'd be leaving soon anyway, and it didn't make much sense to get attached to anything and make it that much harder to leave." She let go of my hand then. "You understand, don't you?"

"Yeah," I answered. "Of course. What else can you do?" I meant to imply that Annetta had more options to consider than simply leaving, but she didn't seem to catch on.

"Not much," she agreed.

"Still..." I said, then didn't know how to finish. I wanted to tell her that we didn't have to assume she would leave when the time came, that we ought to consider the possibility of finding something worth staying for, and that I couldn't help getting attached, that I still wanted to spend as much time with her as I could, that I didn't care about how hard it would be to let go, I still wanted to hold her hand now. "Don't you think maybe..." and again, I didn't know how to finish. It seemed too presumptuous of me to suggest that I might become more important to her than France. It seemed downright ridiculous, in fact, to assume that after only three days....

"No, Spencer, don't even think about it. I'm sure it won't be easy

Courage, Love and the Meaning of Christmas

saying goodbye to you, but let's not make it harder, okay? Please?"

If she hadn't said please, I'd have persisted. I didn't want to be one of those who suffered in silence and did no one any good. But if that's what she wanted, then I'd go along with it, for now. I looked at my watch and it was already 5:30. Time had passed by quickly. "You've got to work in a little while," I said.

Annetta looked at my watch and gasped. "I'm late for dinner!" she said. "I'd better get home quick."

When we opened the door of our room, the library was dark. The doors were locked from the outside but not from the inside. The sky had clouded over and half an inch of new snow had already fallen.

I drove Netta home and she invited me in for dinner, but I told her another time would be better. I knew she'd have to leave for work soon anyway, I didn't want to get stranded with too many strangers at once, and I wasn't sure I would be quite myself with my fresh disappointment and new concern for Grandma.

22 Gone but Not Forgotten

When I got home to Grandma's and walked inside, the house felt lonelier than ever before, and the quiet was too much to take. There was no telling when Grandma would come home from shopping, so I walked to the storage shed attached to the back of the house and found a pair of cross-country skis and boots.

By then, another inch of powder had fallen. The new snow made skiing smooth and comfortable, while the hard crust underneath kept me sliding along quickly. I started off down the road toward town, the hood of my parka pulled over my head and my face lowered to keep the snow out of my eyes. A light wind at my back swirled the snow along at my feet so sometimes when I looked down, I didn't seem to be moving at all.

Soon I found myself caught up in the rhythm of skiing. I stepped forward quickly and simultaneously pushed off with the opposite pole, glided forward for a foot or two, then stepped off onto the other foot and glided again. Light from the bright moon filtered through holes in the clouds here and there, supplying ample light to show me the way.

Before I knew it, I had covered the five miles to town. I hadn't found any solutions to my new dilemmas, but I had found a degree of peace and calm. Solutions would come with time. I would be patient. Three inches of soft, white snow covered the roads now and I could continue through town without taking off the skis. I thought of skiing past Becca's, but didn't know what I'd say to Netta if I saw her.

I skied a few more blocks into town and was about to turn around when I reached the cemetery. Down the road a ways, a pair of car headlights shone through the falling snow as they drove toward me. I preferred not to be seen or talk to anyone just now, so I skied into the cemetery and disappeared between the trees and tombstones. When I reached the back row, I turned left and stopped at a small, shiny granite headstone. After releasing my bindings and laying my poles on the snow, I sat down and leaned one shoulder against it, taking off one glove and tracing the inscription with bare fingers: Andrew Rasmussen, 1934 - 2017.

The flakes had stopped falling and I lay back in the snow, staring up at the heavy clouds rushing by overhead. Bare branches of maple trees stood in stark contrast to the white edges of the clouds and the moon's round, white curves when it managed to break through cracks in the atmosphere's canopy.

The snow felt soft and cool against my back, and I took a deep breath to relax. I wanted to think, to figure everything out, but nothing came to mind. I had long since come to terms with Grandpa's departure, it was Grandma I worried about now.

The moon broke through the clouds just then, and its light poured onto the fresh snow, almost turning the scene to day. I turned my head to watch the transformation, and an ancient, ornate tombstone nearby caught my attention. Corners had long since worn and chipped away, and moss covered half of the lower north side. The inscription read Kowallis, Infant Girl, July 15-24, 1889. I leaned forward and peered closer to read the moss-covered inscription below. "Gone but not Forgotten."

Why do people have to remember? I asked myself. *Why can't they just forget and get on with their lives?* Do we try to remember out of a sense of loyalty? As if we're proving our love for the departed by suffering and grieving and never letting go? The departed couldn't want that — and it certainly doesn't make the living feel any better.

But I can't just forget, either, I realized. I wouldn't want to. Remembering Grandpa made my life richer. He became a part of me, and that part stays forever and adds its bit of sweetness to living.

My head spun. Remembering simultaneously causes pain and makes lives richer. I couldn't make sense of it, couldn't decide which was the best way to react.

I thought about my own life, too, that one day I would be buried in the frozen ground. Would I be forgotten? Would remembering me cause pain? If Grandpa hadn't been such a great person, he would have been easier to let go. But you can't just live your life in mediocrity to avoid future pain — that would only cause more pain. No, like it or not, suffering can not be avoided. Not in this life. Not as long as love and loss and death exist.

So all we need, I thought, is a way to get past the pain, some place to find comfort. I knew where I wanted to find a little comfort right now. I wanted to see Netta. True, she would leave for France soon, but for right now, it felt good to be with her. Even among the living there will be pain, I realized, but when you share it, it becomes more bearable.

"Ah, Grandpa," I sighed to myself, reaching out to touch the cold stone once more. "If only Grandma could have you nearby."

For the third time in three days, the same feeling swept over me. The deep peace, the strength, the hope that touched me and helped me decide to drive to Wyoming early. The feeling after chopping wood in the barn. And now here.

This time I recognized the feeling. It was the same way I felt when Grandpa used to look at me with so much love and pride in his eyes. The same thing I felt when he and Grandma would sing together, hand in hand at the piano. The same feeling as when I knew I was loved and accepted unconditionally.

"Grandpa?" I asked under my breath. "Is that you?" The feeling continued strong inside me and I suddenly felt that everything would be all right. That things would work themselves out just fine. I found it impossible to believe otherwise when the world suddenly felt so right. I sat up in the snow and reached out to touch his tombstone once more. "I love you, too, Grandpa," I whispered softly.

23 Love & Courage

Soon I got up and skied out of the cemetery. I felt better now, so I grew restless to keep moving. A few minutes later I found myself at the concrete bridge between the high school and the café, gazing down into the water. Reflections from the sky shimmered like silver on the ripples, and I remembered the dime I had tossed into the stream two nights ago.

What if I'd have known, I wondered, if I'd have known all along that Netta was leaving soon and that she wouldn't let me get close to her, would I still have made that wish? *I guess that's the danger in making wishes for yourself,* I thought, *they just might come true and you have no one else to blame.*

Anyway, of course I'd have made the same wish. The short amount of time I had spent with Annetta had been wonderful. I had already learned and changed so much, and I couldn't imagine giving that up. My thoughts then took the next logical step: if what we had shared already was good, if the connection was worth any pain it might bring, if we're better off for having crossed paths, then why wouldn't more connection be even better?

Of course! It all comes back to courage—you can't live your life setting up safeguards against getting hurt when you should be acting with courage! You can't hold back when you should be living. Life is far too limited already, too short, too precious to waste, to throw it away, to lock up and hold back and save, when you only get to keep what you spend. I should open up and spend it all, and I should spend it freely, trusting that there will always be more. That's what it means to live.

And that was exactly what I determined to do. Netta could do whatever she wanted with her time and her heart, but I would be myself and not hold back my feelings. I looked up at the sky and tried to guess what time it was, but the clouds offered no clues. Maybe it wasn't too late to catch her at work. I started off immediately toward Becca's and didn't stop until I stood outside the door, looking in through the glass at the dark interior.

The reflection of the street lamp made it difficult to see inside, but I could tell that the kitchen light was still on and that a shadow occasionally moved past it from within. I had no way of knowing whether Netta or Jim cast the shadow but to wait and see if they stepped into the light. Then the light went out.

I stood on the sidewalk looking at my own reflection on the glass then. There was no use trying to hide, I couldn't take off running with these skis on, and I must have been perfectly visible already from the inside, standing under the street lamp outside the large windowpane. So I waited. And then the door opened and Annetta's face peered out.

"Spencer! Have you been here long?" she asked.

"No, I just skied up," I said. "I was hoping to catch you before you went home."

"Well come in then, it's freezing out there!"

Courage, Love and the Meaning of Christmas

I unclipped my ski bindings and walked inside, my boots clicking on the tile floor.

"Aren't you cold?" Netta asked.

"No, I'm okay. As long as you keep moving, you stay warm enough." Even so, I gave a quick shiver, more like a shudder, at the sudden change in temperature.

"Can I get you some hot chocolate?" she asked.

"Yes. Please. That sounds good."

I pulled off my coat and draped it over a bar stool as Netta got two mugs of steaming hot chocolate, each with a dab of whipped cream floating on top. She left the lights off and carried them around the bar.

"Come over here," she directed, walking toward a corner booth. She set the mugs on the table, then walked back to the cash register and took out a few quarters for the juke box.

When the records started playing, she slid in next to me. Here in the corner, we could sit next to each other and still face each other without turning completely sideways. At first, she seemed concerned about how I felt after the news about her leaving, but soon relaxed as she saw I was back to my usual self.

"How was work?" I asked.

Annetta rolled her eyes a little. "Tolerable," she said. She looked tired.

"Why?" I asked. "What happened?"

"Nothing, really," she sighed. "It's just..." she stopped there.

"Ya might as well tell me, Netta," I said.

Annetta gave in and began talking without looking up. "Oh, it's just some of the people around here. They don't mean any harm, but...they don't know what they're doing."

I had no idea what she was talking about, so I waited for her to continue.

"See, Jim's a really nice guy, and the only one near my age around here, and we had sort of been friends from when I used to visit, so when I moved up here and we spent a lot of time together, everyone had us pegged as a couple."

I hadn't worried about Jim as competition since I first got to know Annetta and decided the two of them were on totally different levels. I steeled myself to hear whatever news came next, afraid that Netta's feelings for Jim might be the true reason for her distance toward me.

"But we're just not a good match," she continued as I breathed a sigh of relief, "but that didn't stop some of the local match makers from encouraging him, telling him to just be patient. I think they somehow got the idea that I would settle down and stay here forever." I put one arm around Netta's shoulders, hoping she wouldn't mind. She lay her head on my shoulder and continued.

"So Jim believed them. A few weeks back, he started talking to me about getting serious. I couldn't believe it! We were best friends, but nothing more. I was so surprised that I'm afraid I didn't take it very well." Annetta winced at the memory. "I laughed and told him he was crazy. And, as you might guess, things haven't been very comfortable between us ever since."

"That's too bad," I consoled, relieved to know that nothing worse had happened.

"But that's not the worst of it," Netta continued. "When word got out that we had broken up — that's what everyone called it! Well, some people got mean. They all took Jim's side as if I was wrong and they had any say in the matter. Some people came here to the café more often than usual, but made a point to not talk to me and to not tip. At first, I was furious that anyone would be so vengeful over what shouldn't have been an issue at all, or any of their business, but then I started missing having friends. At least Jim. So I started making an effort to be extra nice, and things are finally getting back to normal, but I'm so tired."

"At least the worst is behind you, right?" I asked hopefully.

Annetta looked up and shook her head. "No," she answered. "Because then you show up, see? And suddenly everybody comes in talking about you and me."

I tried to focus on Annetta's feelings, but couldn't help feel the hope that sentence gave me.

"So much for their loyalty to Jim. By now I couldn't care less what anyone thinks or says, but there's poor Jim, working right beside me, having to listen to every bit of it. It's like everyone just forgot him. And how must that make him feel? To hope and wait all these months for something to happen with me, and then some guy just shows up out of nowhere, and it all works out for him just like that?"

By this time I was soaring. Never had I felt so good before and had to try not to show it. I couldn't believe what I was hearing.

"I mean, I never led him on in the first place, I even told him straight out that it wasn't going to happen, but I know he just kept hoping anyway. Tonight he'd hardly even look at me. I feel awful."

Now she looked so sad that I didn't care what she wanted or didn't want from me. I wrapped my other arm around her and pulled her close. Annetta scooted closer and wrapped one arm across my chest.

Courage, Love and the Meaning of Christmas

"Part of me knew something would happen with you and me right from the beginning," Annetta whispered tiredly. "So I decided right off that I wouldn't let it."

I wondered what, exactly, she was talking about. I wondered if she meant that she was falling for me and why she was trying not to. I wondered what would happen now that she had failed. Or if she had failed.

"You're not blaming yourself for all the trouble with Jim, are you?" I asked. I felt her body relax a little then.

"I guess I shouldn't, should I?"

"I'd say the only part that's your fault is that you're so irresistible." I ran my fingers through her hair and she looked up into my eyes and smiled weakly, then lay her head back on my shoulder.

"Listen, Spencer," she said, "don't think I'm not a little crazy about you, okay? Because I am."

I squeezed her a little closer and felt my heart pounding in my throat.

"I wasn't going to tell you that, either." She laughed a little. "But let's not get involved, okay? I'm leaving so soon and there's no telling if we'll ever even see each other again. Why put ourselves through that? And Jim deserves a little consideration, too. He's been a real gentleman and a true friend. He's earned that much."

"I've been thinking a lot about that since this afternoon," I said, "and I've decided something." I wanted to look her in the eye while I said it, but she didn't look up. "I thought about everything you said about courage and about living life, and I realized that I don't want to pretend I don't like you, and I don't want to miss out on something good that could happen between us. I know I can't make you change your mind, but I had to tell you what I thought and how I feel about you."

"And how do you feel about me, Spencer?"

I wasn't prepared to answer that question. Sure, I really liked her, maybe even loved her, in a way, but it was too early to commit that to words. On the other hand, nothing less would do. Saying "I like you" or "I think you're swell" would sound so weak and meaningless. "I'm crazy about you, too," I finally said, repeating her own words and feeling less vulnerable because of it. "I know we don't know each other all that well and that we don't have much time left to spend together, but when that's gone, I don't want to spend the rest of my life regretting that I never told you, or never held your hand, or never kissed you."

By the time I finished the last sentence, Annetta had looked up from my shoulder. She spun around on the bench so she faced me, then wrapped both arms around my shoulders and buried her face in my neck.

"It wasn't fair for me to ask how you felt," Annetta whispered, "when I already knew I wouldn't change my mind."

"What would change your mind?" I asked.

"Don't ask me that, please," she said. "At least give it more time, okay?"

So I just held her there without a word, hoping something was happening despite all her determination and words and resolutions, hoping I had enough time to make her want to stay.

"Listen," she said after a while, "everyone's going snowmobiling tomorrow. I'd like it if you'd come."

"I'd love to," I answered.

"Good. We're all meeting around eight by the highway."

We slid my skis inside her car from the back and she gave me a ride home. I hugged her once more after taking my skis out of the trunk at Grandma's house. This time she pushed away after a moment, but kept hold of my hands and stood close to me, looking up into my eyes, near enough for me to feel her warm breath on my chin. She looked happy again.

"Listen," she said, "You can call me Annetta if you want. Nobody else calls me that and I like it when you do."

24 Bright Sunshine

I woke up the next morning when the sun shone in through the window and warmed the heavy blankets I had buried myself under. I blinked my eyes and wondered for a moment why I felt so wonderful.

The instant I remembered seeing Annetta last night, I also remembered snowmobiling today. I found my watch on the floor and jumped out of bed instantly when I saw I only had half an hour.

After a quick shower, I found Grandma downstairs with a breakfast of toast and eggs waiting.

"G'morning, Grandma," I said, giving her a hug. "Feels like I haven't seen you in ages. How was shopping?"

"We had a nice time, thank you," Grandma answered. "Where were you all night?"

"I skied in to town. Then Netta gave me a ride home."

Courage, Love and the Meaning of Christmas

Grandma's eyebrows raised a little as a smile spread over her face. I knew she was happy for me. "Does that mean you're joining everyone to go snowmobiling today?" she asked.

"Yeah," I answered. "I'm almost late, as a matter of fact."

"Oh, I wouldn't worry too much," she said. "They never leave quite when they say they will. And I made you lunch."

"You're the best, Grandma!" I said as I shoveled the eggs and toast into my mouth, trying to eat as quickly as possible.

"Will you be taking Grandpa's sled?" she asked.

"Could I? That would be great!"

"Of course you may," Grandma answered. "It's out in the back of the truck, but I don't know if you'll be able to start that old thing."

"I started it the other day. It runs great."

"Then you'll have the fastest snowmobile on the mountain," Grandma said, smiling at my excitement.

It was true. Grandpa's truck was plenty old. "They don't make 'em like they used to," he always said. "Yep, they make 'em better," someone would invariably answer. But he kept it running and in good shape. Grandpa's snowmobile was an entirely different matter. He never pretended that old, boxy sleds were any match for modern technology, and he always chose the best machine money could buy.

I ran upstairs to brush my teeth, then grabbed my waterproof winter clothes, found a helmet in a closet, and ran out the back door after kissing Grandma goodbye.

"We'll talk soon," I promised.

"You go have yourself a good time," she answered, "and be safe."

I tossed everything but the sack lunch in the front seat, then walked to the back of the truck. The snowmobile was beautiful, and I couldn't help stopping to admire it for a moment. I remembered the power of its 900cc engine, the grip of its one-hundred-sixty-inch track with three-inch lugs, and couldn't wait to pull it out of the truck, squeeze the throttle, and feel it fly across the snowfields again.

I put the lunch inside a saddle bag attached to the rear of the snowmobile seat. Inside the bag I also found a thermal foil-coated tarp, half a dozen year-old chemical hand warmers that probably wouldn't work anymore, and a few granola bars, equally old. I grimaced and tossed the granola bars onto the woodpile. I found a half-full gas can that I set in the truck bed, then jumped into the cab and started the engine.

It was already ten past eight, and I hoped I wouldn't miss the group, since I didn't know where we'd be riding. Of course I could always call Andrea to find out.

I flew over the road to town and noticed to my dismay that the wind had drifted away most of the new snow and exposed the old, hard crust. Oh, well, I thought, there will be more powder in the mountains.

I reached the parking lot next to the highway just as everyone began piling into various trucks with a dozen sleds piled on trailers or resting in truck beds. I stopped the truck and stepped out, hoping to locate Netta somewhere in the crowd.

Jim turned around and I saw a smile on his face. It transformed him, and I realized that I probably had misjudged him from our brief encounters at the café. As our eyes met, his smile faded and he gave me a curt nod before turning away.

A few trucks were pulling off onto the road and I had resigned myself to driving up alone when Amy jumped out of a Suburban and ran over. She opened the passenger door and climbed in. "Hey! You ready?" she asked. "Let's get goin'!"

I climbed into the cab and said hi.

"Netta's gotta ride up with Dad," Amy said. "She's getting grilled about you right now." She made a tsk, tsk, tsk sound with her tongue. "You should have gone and met him."

I shrugged my shoulders. "Yeah, I guess so."

"Don't worry about it, though, it's no biggie." Amy spun around and looked the snowmobile over. "Nice machine ya got there. We are gonna have fun!"

By now everyone had begun moving and we pulled out behind Jim's truck onto the highway.

"It's too bad about the whole Netta thing," Amy said. I looked over questioningly and she added, "I mean the whole Jim thing. He's a great guy. I'm sure you'd have gotten along great if not for…you know. The whole Netta thing."

"Yeah, too bad," I agreed, more wholeheartedly than Amy could have known. If not for the whole Jim thing, Netta and I would have had one less barrier between us.

"So, Spence, you much of a snow rider?"

"I've been out a dozen times," I answered. "We usually ride down in the other end of the valley when we come up for Christmas."

"You're gonna love the canyons, then," Amy said. "It's a million times better than the valley. There are tons of areas to choose from with steep hills and drifts and everything. You'll see."

Courage, Love and the Meaning of Christmas

"Sounds great, I'm glad I came."

Amy picked up my gloves, gators, and pant shells from the floor and set them on the seat beside her. "Nice gear," she said. "You sure you're not a serious rider?"

"Yeah. I mostly use that for cross-country skiing and back country stuff."

"Really? Ever been on any serious treks?"

"Not really," I answered. "I mostly just go for a few hours at a time. I usually camp once or twice each winter, though."

"In snow caves?"

"Sometimes. Usually we just bring a tent unless we know somewhere where other people have already dug caves. They take a long time."

"It seems like snow caves would be cold," Amy said.

"They're actually pretty warm inside. The air stays above freezing if you build it right. Once I got caught in a blizzard about fifteen miles from my car. I didn't have a tent, so I decided to dig a snow cave under a drift with the back of my ski. By the time I had it big enough to crawl into, it was probably 3:00 a.m. and I was soaked. Once I stopped digging, I got cold, and ended up just skiing through the storm back to the car anyway."

"Sounds like fun!" Amy said enthusiastically. "Sounds beautiful."

"It's kind of funny now," I admitted, "but I felt miserable then. I got pretty cold."

"Well, it's a beautiful, sun-shiny day today," Amy said, and reached up to turn on the radio. The truck only had an AM radio, and Amy turned it up loud enough for the music to begin to distort. We found enough songs we knew to sing along with for most of the drive.

Sometimes I would glance over at this bundle of energy and enthusiasm sitting beside me. Her presence felt like rays of warm, bright sunshine powerful enough to cheer up even the most determined pessimist. I was surprised to realize that I automatically loved this girl much the same way I had naturally fallen for her older sister.

When we reached the snow-covered parking lot in the mountains, we backed up to a snow pile where a plow had pushed it. Jim walked over and helped me pull the sled out without a word. "You sure you can handle this machine?" he asked.

"I'll do my best," I affirmed.

I filled the gas tank and opened the fuel line, opened the choke, and pressed the starter button. The engine turned over a few times slowly, then stopped. The battery was drained, so I'd have to use the starting cord. I gave it several pulls with no results.

Most of the other sleds had been unloaded and a few of them were already sputtering and roaring as their riders drove them out of the way.

I gave the cord another pull, and heard Jim yell from across the parking lot, "You sure you can handle that machine?" I looked up and waved a bit, feeling a bit timid and hoping it would start soon. He laughed and started up his own machine.

Netta finished putting on her bibs and boots and headed my way. I pulled harder, hoping this time it would go. I heard it almost fire, I thought. Jim rode his machine over to me half standing, half kneeling on his sled. He got off, walked over to my machine, and lifted up on the kill switch which I had forgotten to check. He gave a quick pull on the cord and the engine instantly roared to life.

"There ya go," he said, smiling.

"Oh, yeah," I said sheepishly. "Thanks."

He nodded at Netta, still walking our way, and drove off.

Netta walked up close to me but didn't give me a hug. "You'd better get dressed quick," she said.

"Why's that?" I asked.

"Cause if you don't, you're gonna lose our race," she smiled. "Good to see ya."

"Good to see you, too," I answered. "I'd love to talk, but I have to get dressed for a race."

When I had pulled on my gear, I turned to find Netta sitting on Grandpa's sled waiting.

"Are you driving mine for the race?" I asked.

"That's right," she answered. "The race was for the driver's seat. Climb on."

I sat down on the seat behind Netta and wrapped one arm around her waist, gripping the seat strap with the other hand, and Netta hit the throttle.

The sled jolted forward while spitting a rooster tail of ice and packed powder out behind us. The powerful engine roared as we accelerated, rocketing ahead toward the powder-covered hills. We were instantly away from the parking lot and began passing other sleds which moved at a more conservative pace. Now I was grateful for the sled's extra-long track and deep tread as we glided easily over the soft surface. Other sleds struggled to maintain speed and avoid bogging down in the deep powder.

It wasn't long before we had passed everyone. A cold wind blew in through my open visor, and the trees and ridges blurred as my eyes watered. The combination of cold, speed, and beauty made me feel more awake and alert than I had in months. The snowmobile rose and fell over the uneven contours of the narrow valley below us, and I let go of the strap and wrapped both arms around Netta's waist. I felt awake and happy.

Annetta maneuvered smoothly between loosely-spaced pines, and I leaned hard left with her as we took a sharp turn up to the top of a low ridge. Along the crest, a narrow path opened between the trees, sometimes barely wide enough for our sled to pass through without whipping us in the face with the needles, weighed down with new snow.

I looked forward down the ridge and saw that it opened up into a wide clearing about fifty yards away. The distance was passing quickly, and the nearer we grew, the more it appeared that the trail ended with a cliff. I felt confident that Netta would see it and didn't say anything, but held a little tighter anyway, getting ready for another abrupt turn.

By the time I realized she wasn't turning, it was too late to do anything about it. She had veered slightly to one side, but we still shot over the edge into utterly empty air. Gravity vanished. Only Netta's firm grip on the handlebars and my hold around her waist kept us from floating away into space. The roar of the engine lessened momentarily as we plummeted through space with the soft whistle of wind blowing through open helmet visors.

The world and sound returned as we made a smooth, steep landing in soft powder. Our helmets knocked together and Netta opened the throttle all the way up again. We must have dropped only five or ten feet, but that had given me enough time to wonder whether or not I should jump clear.

We scooted across the half-mile wide clearing, and my adrenaline was still pumping as she brought us to a stop in the center and killed the engine.

"Having fun?" Netta asked, pulling off her helmet and spinning sideways on the seat to look in my eyes.

"Sure am," I answered, "but I'm going to have to dock you for that improper left turn, failure to signal, and this has got to be the sloppiest parallel parking job I've ever seen."

"You mean I don't get my license?" she asked with a shocked

expression.

"I'm sorry, Miss. It's going to be a while before we can turn you loose on the streets. It wouldn't be safe!" I pulled off my own helmet and added, "I assume you knew about the cliff?"

"Yeah," she added. "I've only gone off it a couple times, but I couldn't resist. Did I scare you?"

"What, that little thing? I hardly noticed."

"Scared me, too," Annetta admitted. She leaned back against me and sighed. "Beautiful, no?"

It was. The meadow stretched away a hundred and fifty yards in every direction across perfectly flat ground, sloping up slightly around the edges and becoming steep mountain sides or tree-covered ridges with narrow canyons leading up and out in every direction.

"There's a shallow lake underneath us," Netta told me. "It's frozen solid right now."

In the distance, the high-pitched whine of snow machines grew nearer. The first sleds appeared behind us, apparently having followed our track, but most of them slowed and skirted the edge of the cliff as they emerged from the trees. One or two took timid leaps from the cliff edge where they dropped three or four feet.

"This place will be full of snowmobiles in a minute," Annetta said. "Let's go." She stood up and stepped around behind me. I slid forward and started the engine.

"Ready?" I asked after we put our helmets back on.

Annetta held on tight. "Let's go," she said.

The smooth powder felt even better from the driver's seat. I made a large loop around the clearing first to enjoy the glassy feeling of the powder, then randomly chose one of the half dozen canyons and the clearing disappeared behind us. Annetta's arms stayed tight around my waist and chest as we flew through snow-covered pines and up and down the narrow canyon walls.

The canyon floor widened at one point, and I saw a small drift running along the top ridge, about fifty feet up. I drove up the opposite canyon wall, then made a slow turn to conserve our speed and charged the opposite mountain. When we reached the top, we still had just enough speed to send us crashing through the soft curl of new snow.

Even ducking behind the short windshield didn't protect us from the pile of snow that tumbled over our heads. A few flakes made their way inside my coat collar and melted against my neck. Netta loved it.

"Do it again!" she said between laughs.

Courage, Love and the Meaning of Christmas

We continued over the ridge and stopped before diving into the next canyon. Atop the far side sat a six-foot cornice, not all of which had been formed by last night's storm. The older snow wouldn't be as soft.

"What do you think?" I asked.

"I don't think we'd make it through that one," she replied.

I lowered my visor like a knight ready for a round of jousting, and without so much as asking if she was ready, I hit the gas and charged down into the canyon. I kept the throttle squeezed tight all the way across the canyon floor and headed straight up the other side.

"Spencer, don't do it!" Netta screamed. "Spencer!"

Twenty feet before the cornice, I steered us gently to the left, turning us around slowly and avoiding the drift. We probably could have reached out and touched the overhanging snow as it passed by to our right, and then we came barreling back downward.

"How did you like that?" I asked when we came to a stop. Netta reached up and opened my visor without a word. The next thing I knew, I had a face full of snow as she packed it into my helmet with her other hand.

I pulled off my helmet as she continued to throw snow in my face, then grabbed her and pushed her off the back of the sled. She held her own well for not being able to see once I had packed a few handfuls of snow into her helmet. We were both on the ground wrestling in the snow when another sled pulled up next to us. We hadn't heard it coming over the sputter of our own idling engine.

"You two stuck?" the driver asked.

"No, we're fine," I answered, water dripping down my face. "I just got something in my eye and had to stop."

Annetta sat up and pulled off her helmet, clearing the snow out of her eyes. "Hi, Dad," she said. "This is Spencer."

Mr. Hall looked me over for a second. I began feeling more than a little uncomfortable. This probably wasn't the way most fathers would prefer to meet their daughters' dates, rolling around on the ground like that.

"I've heard a lot about you," he finally said, extending his hand.

"I've heard a little about you, too," I answered, shaking it and wishing I had heard a little more.

"You better watch out," he said, then looked over at his daughter. *This does not sound good*, I thought. I looked over at Annetta, her grinning face still dripping wet, and Mr. Hall continued, "or this little girl'll catch you off guard."

"So I've learned," I answered, and breathed a sigh of relief that I wasn't in trouble.

"That's right!" Annetta shouted, jumping up with an armful of snow meant for her father's face. Mr. Hall caught her before she could get solid footing for her attack and held her tight, her arms pinned between them.

"Truce?" he asked. Annetta thought it over, still grinning. She looked like a little girl there, playing so easily with her father. With me, she had always seemed so independent and grown up. Now I saw the childish playful side of her emerge. Mr. Hall began to smile, too, apparently making his own plans for the snow battle.

"Truce! Truce!" Annetta suddenly cried, suing for peace. But it was too late. Mr. Hall's six-foot-plus frame easily picked Annetta up and set her down in the snow. He barely managed to hold her in place there while his other hand scooped snow onto her face.

"Spencer! Help!" she shouted, giggling and laughing almost too hard to speak.

I knelt down in the snow beside them and scooped enough snow over to cover her face completely. She stopped struggling then, and Mr. Hall let go of her. She just lay there for a moment, then sat up, the snow piling into her lap.

"What I meant," she clarified, "was to help *me*."

"Oh, sorry for the misunderstanding," I apologized.

We all stood up and brushed ourselves off, then sat sidesaddle on our parallel sleds.

"Beautiful day, isn't it?" Mr. Hall asked.

"Sure is," I agreed. "And these mountains are spectacular."

"That's correct," said Mr. Hall, as if their beauty were scientific rather than artistic. "Do you know how mountains are formed?"

I suddenly felt like a student in class. Perhaps his appreciation really was academic. "When plates of the earth's crust clash?" I ventured.

"Correct. In most cases, one tectonic plate is forced down while the other rises over it. The range around Amber is unusual in that as the plates came together, both plates were forced upward above the plain. Don't you think that's fascinating?"

"Yeah, that's interesting," I said, and looked around to compare the nearby ridges to other mountains I had known, but couldn't tell the difference.

When I looked back at Mr. Hall, our eyes met, and I was instantly struck by the impression that I knew him, really knew him, much like

Courage, Love and the Meaning of Christmas

my experience with Netta the other night, but even stronger.

He seemed comfortable and confident, his mind open and inquisitive. Intelligence and acceptance seemed to radiate from him. I sensed his sincere interest in the world and in people, his genuine perspective that life is fun and joyful. I felt sure that whenever he met someone new, that he turned it into a win-win situation, and both people were uplifted.

So that's where the girls get it, I thought, and I wondered what their mother was like. I would ask later on, I decided, and I could hardly wait to meet her.

"I'm sure we'll see each other a lot more now that we've been introduced," he stated. I couldn't tell whether that sounded more like an invitation or a command.

"I'm sure we will," I agreed. "That sounds good. Do you want to ride with us?" I offered.

"Sure, for a minute, till whenever we get separated," he answered. "Or until you can't keep up. But I'll see you back at the clearing for lunch. Meet at two o'clock."

Mr. Hall straddled his snowmobile again and took off up the canyon. Netta and I picked up our helmets to empty the snow from them and sat down next to each other along the snowmobile seat.

"Your dad seems like a pretty cool guy," I said.

"I knew you'd like him," Annetta answered. "I knew he'd like you, too."

"What made you so sure?"

"Cause he looks right into the center of you. And he sees what's in there. And if you have a good heart, then..." Annetta's voice trailed off here. She seemed to be thinking of something else as she finished the sentence, "...he loves you."

"That's amazing," I said. In her expression, I caught a glimpse of the clouded look she always got just before telling me that we shouldn't get involved. "Are you driving now or me?" I asked, anxious to move her attention away from that thought before it led anywhere.

Netta looked up at me without answering, the troubled expression still spreading across her face. This was not a discussion I would win with words, I knew. Instead, I stood up and stepped over the snowmobile seat then sat down again facing the opposite direction. I reached out and pulled her tight against me. She hugged me back weakly for a moment, then a little stronger.

"Thanks," she said, letting go and pulling her helmet on. "You drive."

25 The Greatest Fear

Annetta and I rode back to the parking lot and picked up her snowmobile. As much as I liked having her arms wrapped around me, driving was a lot easier and more fun with only one person per sled.

We got stuck a few times when the track dug deep into the snow, and digging out proved an exhausting exercise, but it gave us a chance to sit and talk for a few minutes while we rested up and cooled off.

As we joked and laughed and talked and told stories, I was amazed to realize that my old self-consciousness, my old panic that I would run out of things to say or, worse, say something stupid and make a fool of myself, seemed completely gone. At least for now. At least with Annetta.

"I've wasted too much of my life," I confided.

"What do you mean?" Annetta inquired.

"I used to be so shy and afraid," I explained, omitting the fact that I was referring to everything before last week. "I missed out on so much because I never even tried, but if I had tried, I'm sure I'd have failed anyway because I was so afraid of failing."

"Hm," Annetta simply replied, looking and trying to imagine a shy, scared version of me.

I wanted to tell her the rest. I wanted her to know how much she had changed me. But I didn't dare. The old me had not completely vanished, and I was afraid that if she knew that part of me, that she would lose any interest in me, and I would lose any chance of wearing down her walls and possibly, maybe, hopefully establishing a long-term relationship.

No, I would keep up the confidence act until it became real. Until it became complete. Until, hopefully, Annetta fell for me completely and we lived happily ever after.

"Come over here," I said, patting the seat with my hand.

"I want to," Annetta admitted, "but I don't want to."

"Explain," I requested.

"You already know, Spencer," she said. "You know I like you more than I want to, and you know I can't get as close to you as I'd like or it will make it harder to leave next month."

"And you know," I countered, "that I don't care about that. I want to live courageously and not miss out on any more living. Especially when I find something as good as you."

"So you're not going to cooperate?" she asked, looking mildly

Courage, Love and the Meaning of Christmas

annoyed.

"I'm afraid not," I said apologetically.

"All right," she began after a brief pause, "I'll answer your question from the other night. I'll tell you what I'm most afraid of." She stomped a more comfortable shelf in the snow for her feet and leaned against her stuck snowmobile's seat, settling in for what could take a while. "Have you ever broken your heart?" she asked.

"No," I answered.

"Well I have, several times, and it's not fun."

I nodded, considering the information respectfully, but not yet feeling swayed.

"Afterward, it's like being buried underground where you can barely breathe and hardly move."

I had to admit that didn't sound fun.

"The last time," she continued, "it took so long to dig my way back up to the surface, that I finally learned my lesson."

"What lesson was that?" I asked, though I already had a pretty good idea.

"To not risk it again," she answered decisively. When she saw the perplexed look appearing on my face, the one that asked if she really intended to live the rest of her life without love, she added, "I mean to manage the risks very carefully. To move forward very slowly, and not get involved that way when, for example, I know I can only be with someone for a few weeks."

"Hm," I simply replied. I had to admit it sounded reasonable. I wished I had some sort of powerful argument why she should open up to me anyway, but I didn't. In fact, I was afraid that she had convinced me that I should respect her boundaries.

"Then again," she said slowly, thoughtfully, staring at me intently....

I waited for her to continue, but not eagerly, barely interested in what she might say next. What more could she say that would matter? The question seemed settled and she had won and I lost.

"I never planned," she began again slowly, "to meet anyone quite like you."

What?! Did I hear right?!

"I didn't plan to tell you that part," she revealed immediately, appearing annoyed at herself for letting it slip out.

But now I knew the truth. Annetta liked me. She *really* liked me. Maybe she even loved me, just a little, or at least had begun to. Part of her wanted to break down those old walls, break her rule and take a chance. Otherwise she never would have let the last part slip out.

And if that was true, then…maybe…maybe she wanted me to….

I stood up and walked over to her sled, then sat down next to her and put an arm around her shoulders. I wanted her to turn toward me and return my embrace. I wanted to feel her warm cheek against mine, her hot breath against my neck. She buried her face in her gloves for a moment and shook her head.

"Spencer, no," she finally said, her resolve winning over her doubts. "No," she repeated more firmly, looking into my eyes this time, then away toward the horizon.

"Don't," she added when I didn't remove my arm from her shoulder. "I've made up my mind. It's the smart thing to do. I'll be glad later. I'm sorry, but I have to watch out for myself first.

"Let's go," she continued quickly, "let's ride some more." She stepped over her seat and hit the starter button, burying any chance of further conversation in the roar of her engine.

26 Passion

The day grew warm and cloudless bluebird skies created an irresistible cheerfulness that eased my disappointment at Annetta's decision not to get closer. After another hour of riding through the beautiful mountains, I was even getting used to the idea of just staying close friends and nothing more.

I could hardly complain, after all! I would spend another week or two – perhaps several hours per day – with a beautiful, interesting girl who really liked me, and that had already transformed me in miraculous ways. Who could say how much more I would improve by the time I went back to school and she flew away around the world?

By the time we headed back to the central clearing for lunch, I felt extremely lucky and grateful for our mostly-platonic relationship.

We raced across the wide open expanse and pulled up next to Mr. Hall and Amy. They both sat on their sled seats backwards, using the rest of the seat as a table, and we caught the end of their conversation.

"I don't know, Dad," Amy said. "It was fun, but it doesn't seem like the thing for me."

"Do you think you'll do another one?" Mr. Hall asked.

Amy thought for a moment. "Yeah, maybe. I don't know! We'll see."

"Talking about the play?" Annetta asked.

Courage, Love and the Meaning of Christmas

"Yeah," Amy answered. "Dad's trying to figure out my life again. Do you think I should become an actress?"

"Do you want to?" Annetta asked.

"How come I knew you'd say that?" Amy complained. "Yes. No. Maybe. How am I supposed to know that after one play?"

"You're not. If you like it enough to do another one, then do another one and decide later."

"Yeah, but what if I do another one," Amy explained, "and I like it, then how do I know that there's not something else I'd like even better?"

"Try a little of everything. Figure it out a little at a time," Annetta said.

"Yeah, that did you a lot of good, big sister. You got a degree in liberal arts and you still don't know what you want to do."

"I want to do everything," Annetta retorted. "That's different."

"Yeah, that sounds even *more* confusing."

"Well there's no hurry," Netta pointed out. "I have time."

"Why don't you go back to school and get a masters degree in liberal arts?" Amy asked.

"There's no such thing," Annetta answered.

"Hm, I wonder why?" Amy added sarcastically. "What do *you* think, Spencer? Am I cut out to be an actress?"

I finished chewing my bite of sandwich and swallowed. "Absolutely. If you don't become an actress, the theatrical world will never be the same."

Amy smiled happily at that. "Yeah, but what about all the other worlds? Are you sure I should be an actress?"

"I'm positive," I affirmed. "I've never been so sure of anything in my life."

Amy frowned once she recognized my exaggeration. "Okay, okay," she conceded, "I get the point. I just thought the answers would be easier to find."

"If you always do what you want to be doing," Annetta said, "then you'll always be doing what you want to be doing."

"What about you, Spencer?" Mr. Hall asked. "What are your plans?"

"Yeah," Amy said. "You have a real major, you must have it all figured out."

"You're an English major, aren't you?" Mr. Hall asked. "Are you planning to teach?"

"That might be okay," I answered. "I don't really know what I'll do, either, but I think I'd like to write."

"Really? What kinds of things would you write?"

"I don't have that all figured out yet," I answered. "Something fun to read, hopefully, and something that could make a difference for the world. Anyway, writing's so competitive and risky, so I guess I'll have to find something else to do officially."

"Well whatever you decide," Mr. Hall said, "make sure to use your talents and passions. They were given to you for a reason, and that's where you'll find the true pay offs."

"Yeah, unless your talents and passions happen to be teaching," Amy said. "That doesn't pay much, does it Daddy?"

Mr. Hall looked at her and smiled wryly. "True, true," he admitted. "But can you imagine what the world would be like if the schools were filled with talented teachers who were passionate about teaching and about their students?"

I reflected for a moment on what my talents and passions might be. I loved the outdoors, for one, but couldn't think of how that might translate into a career. I liked to write, to examine and analyze, to learn, and then share what I learned. That sounded a lot like teaching. I liked my friends, I liked growing happier and more courageous. I liked pumpkin pie and hot chocolate.

The more I thought about it, the less my interests seemed like a useful compass to choose a career.

"So how do you recognize your talents and passions?" I asked.

Mr. Hall's eyes lit up at the chance to explain what was clearly a favorite topic – though it seemed altogether possible that he had dozens of them. "That's easy," he began, "just look back and observe what you enjoy doing and what you seem to have a knack for, or what you always seem to do well. Also, look for what gets you excited, what you could do all day long and never get tired of."

"I can see how that would make a career more enjoyable."

"Most 'work' involves negative feedback loops," Mr. Hall continued. "Most people work out of necessity. They need food, shelter, and entertainment, which puts their life in the negative, so they seek money. As soon as they have some money, they pay the bills, all needs are met, and they're back at zero, which is good enough until more needs arise.

"When you work from your passions and talents, you're working with positive feedback loops. You do something you enjoy, and that moves you toward a positive balance, and you want even more. You

Courage, Love and the Meaning of Christmas

may feel satisfied, and you may always stay happily in the black, but you never get 'enough.' There's always more to enjoy; to do, to learn, to discover, to teach and share. It's a fantastic way to spend your life."

"I get it," I said, nodding my head, "but does anyone really find a job like that that never gets old?"

"Well," admitted Mr. Hall, "most jobs have multiple facets to them, and not all of them may match your passions and talents. You may love teaching but dislike grading. You may love to travel and see new places and meet new people, but also crave stability."

"You may love acting but also love marine biology and writing and travel and languages and dance and hiking," Annetta said, looking at Amy.

"You may love bread pudding but also love Spencer," Amy shot back sarcastically. I laughed and Netta returned what might best be described as a gentle glare, as if to say 'don't encourage her.'

"Well?" I asked. "*Do* you love bread pudding?"

"Also," Mr. Hall added, "You don't have to match all your talents and passions to your job, but make sure you find some time for them at least in your free time. Unused talents tend to demand attention by making you feel restless and unfulfilled."

A light went off in my head. "So talents and passions have a lot to do with leading a meaningful life," I thought out loud.

"Yes," Mr. Hall agreed, "exactly."

"And they're different for everyone," I continued.

"Of course."

"And that's why there's no one single universal key to the Meaning of Life," I concluded.

"Well," Mr. Hall began, "talents and passions are one key, but there must be others, too."

"Okay, Dad," Amy sighed, "we know courage will come into the conversation, so let's get it over with."

"Yes," Mr. Hall agreed, "once you've found your talents and passions, it takes courage to act on them. Courage to go forward without knowing everything yet. Take things day by day, moment by moment. Trust that the way will open to you."

"All right!" Amy exclaimed, "Passion and talents, check. Courage, check. Riding snowmobiles before all the snow melts, nope. It looks like our work is cut out for us!" She stood up and stretched, then sat down and started her machine. "You guys coming?" she asked as she donned her helmet.

The rest of us stood up and packed our lunches back in the sleds. Once we had put on our helmets and started our engines, the four of us charged off in single file toward a new canyon. We rarely stopped to talk, but sometimes followed each other when someone found a good jump or hill to climb. Sometimes one of our sleds would get stuck in the powder and we would all dig and pull together to get it free. It was exhausting work, but easier than doing it alone. Sometimes we would separate, crossing over low ridges into other canyons and drainages, and not see each other for minutes at a time.

I found a small clearing hemmed in with a few small aspens and tall pine trees and stopped in the middle. I hadn't seen anyone else for ten or fifteen minutes. I shut off the engine to listen for the sound of their sleds and determine which direction I should go next. What I heard took me completely by surprise.

The silence of this little patch of sunlight stood out in such calm contrast to the screaming engines I had listened to all day long that I almost held my breath to avoid disturbing it. The soft powder lay unbroken around me except for my single track coming in, and blue tree shadows rested unmoving, unflinching on its surface. The trees stood perfectly still and straight, and it struck me that this is all they did; day in, day out, for fifty or a hundred years or more. It charmed me, and I decided to try it for just a few minutes and see how it felt.

I took off my helmet and lay down along the snowmobile seat, staring up at the blue, blue sky, letting the peace work its way inside. Nature was my passion.

I wanted this day to last forever. I wanted Christmas vacation to last forever. I didn't want Annetta to move away, and I didn't want to end up gone and forgotten. But there was no use thinking about that now. My family would be here in a few days. I'd introduce Netta to everyone and build as many ties as possible. I'd try to make this a lasting relationship and discover where it might go from there. That was the best I could do.

For now, I would simply enjoy myself as much as possible. I would breathe deep and close my eyes to better appreciate the silence.

27 Lost

I don't know how long I slept, but when my eyes opened, the scene had changed. The tree tops waved back and forth gently in a cold wind.

Courage, Love and the Meaning of Christmas

The shadows had vanished—or taken over—as darkening clouds raced across the sky. I shivered and sat up.

Somewhere far away, the buzz of a lone snowmobile sounded like a housefly. The clearing had lost its charm, and I started my snowmobile, anxious to find my way back to the others. I turned myself around to head back the way I came, then looked over my shoulder. I wondered how far back these mountains go. Probably a hundred miles without another human being.

Snow began to fall in flurries. I reached the place where I had come down a steep ridge into this narrow canyon, but didn't follow my meandering tracks, wanting to get back as quickly as possible. The path between trees grew narrow enough that I had to slow down. I hoped I wouldn't get stuck anywhere so tight that I couldn't go forward and couldn't turn around.

For that matter, I hoped I was going the right direction to take me back to the big clearing. I hadn't kept careful track of the little twists and turns I had followed all afternoon, and with the clouds covering the sky now, I couldn't use the sun to determine my direction.

I looked up and watched which way the clouds blew past the tree tops, trying to remember how that related to the sun's earlier position, then gave up. I knew I could go back and retrace my tracks if I had to.

When I found a low, sloping hill to my left, I buzzed up and over it, and was rewarded with a wider, more open canyon to follow. I squeezed the throttle harder and felt the cold wind press against my chest and circulate through my helmet.

I dropped down a short, steep hill, catching air over a heavy six-foot tall drift at the summit, then zooming down into a wide, open clearing. In the center stood the tallest pine I had seen all day. It must have been well over a hundred years old. Its lower branches reached out and formed a circus-tent-like opening with bare ground exposed below.

A single sled track ran through the center of the meadow, and I wondered who had made it and how long ago and which direction they were going as worries about getting myself lost nibbled at the edge of my mind.

Another five minutes brought me to more tracks and the surroundings began to look familiar. I occasionally shut off the engine to listen for other snow machines, but heard only silence and the wind moaning through the pines. The day had grown dark, the snow fell thicker, and I raced on quickly.

Ten minutes later, the snow was falling hard in quarter-size flakes.

The large flakes indicated a big storm, with plenty of moisture to dump as a warm, wet high-pressure and cold low-pressure systems collided.

By the time I reached the central clearing, no one remained and three inches of new snow covered most of the day's tracks. I continued up the canyon toward the parking lot ducked behind the windshield with my helmet visor closed.

Dropping temperatures took some of the fun out of riding and I could feel a dull ache in my arms and shoulders from the day's exertions. It was dark enough now that the sun must have been dropping over the horizon. I didn't regret that the day had ended as I reached the parking lot and found most of the other sleds already loaded in trucks and on trailers.

No one seemed to have left yet. I stopped my sled behind Grandpa's truck and walked toward the other cars to find Annetta and see if she would ride home with me. Mr. Hall and Jim were talking near a trailer and I overheard their conversation as I approached.

"I'm going back to find her," Mr. Hall said. I noticed the concerned look on his face, and Jim turned to me.

"What's up?" I asked him.

"Amy's not back. We're going to look for her. Wait here."

Jim turned his back and helped Mr. Hall drag his sled from the trailer, then jogged away toward his own machine.

The picture of the single track in the snow in the unfamiliar clearing with the giant pine tree flashed through my mind. Along with the image came the overwhelming feeling I had experienced in the cemetery and two other times this week, only this time instead of peace, I felt urgency. A calm voice inside my head, louder than I had ever heard my own thoughts, shouted "GO!"

The voice frightened me. Adrenaline poured into my veins and my heart raced. I looked around the parking lot and could barely see through the thick snowflakes filling the air. It occurred to me that the situation was serious. People die in storms like this, and there was no telling how long it would last.

I didn't know the territory well and I had only a few pieces of the winter survival gear I should have carried with me. If I had planned for a ski outing, I'd be prepared. I'd have enough food and water and clothing and gear to survive for days. But I didn't. I should just stay here. If I got myself stuck or lost, I would only endanger the others who would come looking for me.

I looked down the canyon leading back to the clearing and the

Courage, Love and the Meaning of Christmas

urgency would not go away. It would not listen to reason. Panic welled up in my throat as I realized that the decision had already been made. I would listen to the voice. I would go back out into the storm. I would look for the clearing with the old tree.

I pushed my fears to the back of my mind and jogged toward my snowmobile. I turned the key and the warm engine roared to life. I hit the gas and snow spewed out behind me as I spun around and headed down the canyon without looking back.

Quarter-size flakes fell everywhere, and the cold wind blew them across the ground before me. My headlight barely pierced twenty feet into the storm, but this part of the path was familiar now, and I skipped along at forty miles per hour, just slowly enough to dodge the small pines that periodically appeared before me.

I reached the meadow and pushed the sled even faster to the other side, then started up a canyon, dodging trees that appeared out of the storm. After riding about a mile, realized I had picked the wrong canyon. I spun around quickly and headed back down.

By the time the meadow came back into view, the drifting snow had all but obliterated even my own recent tracks. I took the next canyon and pushed on, hoping to spot a familiar landmark.

Twenty minutes later found me back in the meadow, trying the third canyon on that end of the clearing. This had to be the one. Unless Amy was lucky enough to find her way out or at least find good shelter, a storm like this could kill her. The thick curtain of falling snow would disorient her. The wind chill would drop the temperatures below zero and if she got wet, she would lose heat even faster. Within hours, she could freeze to death.

I had no idea what had become of Mr. Hall and Jim, so I couldn't count on them. If I didn't find Amy in this canyon…I wouldn't know what else to do.

The snow grew deeper by the minute— two or three feet in some places where the wind blew it into drifted piles—and the dropping temperatures made it light and fluffy. Even Grandpa's sled with its long track and deep lugs was beginning to bog down and nearly get stuck in the deepest spots if I didn't keep up my speed.

I rode on through the storm, wondering what I would do when, or if, I found Amy. I remembered the voice in my head, though, and put any thought of failure out of my mind.

Perhaps five minutes later, I was rewarded with a familiar sight. Up ahead I spotted the tall pine tree. The single track had run through this ravine, and I had seen this place in my mind when the voice told me to move. I sped through the clearing, wondering where to look now that I had found my way here.

Just as I passed the tree, I noticed an irregular-shaped bump in the snow that had not been there before. My headlight illuminated the shape as it drew near, and I recognized the outline of a snowmobile's large front end and long seat. It looked half buried, its nose pointing upward, its track submerged and stuck in the snow.

I cranked the handlebars hard left, narrowly avoiding an impact with the tail of the sled. Before me now I saw the steep hill and I was struck with an idea of what to do next. Before I had time to consider the outcome, I squeezed the throttle hard and charged toward the hill with all the speed I could gather.

I couldn't see a thing at this speed. The snowflakes came at me in long, white streaks as if I were about to jump to light speed. When I hit the hillside abruptly, moving at least fifty miles per hour, it nearly bounced me from the seat, but I gripped the handlebars tightly and continued squeezing the throttle all the way open.

Somewhere above me in the darkness, the giant cornice loomed. This time I would not turn to the side and dodge it. I was playing chicken with a stationary object, and I had a pretty good idea which of us was about to win. I only hoped my plan would work. The headlight illuminated a dim white mass through the storm. I held on for half a second longer, then jumped.

Above the sound of snow in my ears as I tumbled up the steep hill through deep, soft powder, came a sickening thud and crunch as the sled embedded itself in the hard drift. It was louder than I had expected as the fiberglass engine cowling cracked and the plastic windshield shattered.

I jumped to my feet, looking up, ears sharp, listening and watching through the storm for any sound or sign of snow tumbling down, thinking for the first time that the crash could cause the entire cornice to break away and slide, crushing and burying me in the process.

The engine had killed on impact. Only the rushing sound of wind and the crystal tinkling of drifting snow against my coat met my ears. Again, I was struck by the peace and beauty of the scene, but this time I couldn't afford the luxury of stopping to enjoy it.

I scrambled up the slope and grabbed the back of the snowmobile. The force of the crash had buried it over half way into the drift. I braced myself as well as I could and pulled backward. The sled didn't budge an inch.

I tugged and pulled and jerked with all my strength against the sled but made no headway, it was lodged in solid, I had gone too fast. I stopped and leaned against the sled, breathing hard, looking down toward the pine tree where Amy must be huddled.

"Dear God," I whispered, "I could use a little help here." It was no use trying to see above the clouds this time. *I know you can hear me.* "I've gotten myself into a bit of trouble, I'm afraid. Could you help me move this snowmobile?" *I don't know what I'll do if I can't move this thing.* I took two deep breaths and started pulling again.

Minutes later, I was hot and winded. I leaned against the sled again, then let myself fall to the snow to catch my breath. I hadn't budged it an inch. It was hopeless. I had no chance of dragging it from the drift. Why did I think of this crazy idea in the first place, and why did I follow through without stopping to reconsider first? I couldn't even get solid footing in the soft snow. I glanced sideways to survey the useless damage I had caused to the wonderful machine, and a new idea hit me square in the face.

I rolled over and started digging and scooping snow from beneath the sled, pushing it out and down the hill. Soon part of the track was hanging free. I stood again and yanked on the seat. This time it moved. Less than half an inch, but it moved. *Thank you, God!*

I dug at the snow below the snowmobile again, then set my feet and pulled for all I was worth, pulling and heaving with all my weight until the sled began to break free. Soon it came a foot at a time, and then it was out, laying up the slope under my new snow cave.

I crawled into the cave and used my gloved hands to dig and scrape the floor flat. I punched holes into the back of the cave, then removed entire blocks of snow at a time. The snow piled easily out the hole below me, and twenty minutes later, the cave had grown barely large enough to fit two people tightly inside.

After backing out of the cave, I ran down the hill, following my tracks back to the tree. I ducked below its massive lower branches and sure enough, there sat Amy huddled against the trunk, balled up tight and shivering.

"What happened?" Amy asked, looking up with glazed eyes. "It sounded like you crashed." Her speech came out slurred and slow.

"I did," I said, happy and relieved to see her.

"Some rescue this is," she said, smiling through chattering teeth.

"C'mon," I said, "I've got a place all set up for us."

"I'm gonna stay here," she said slowly. "It's warmer here."

Amy was slipping into the middle stages of hypothermia. The freezing ground and wind that made its way through these branches had lowered her core body temperature enough to slow her thinking and slur her speech. A few hours longer and she would have frozen for sure - her body was already losing its ability to generate heat. If she stopped shivering, that's when I'd really start worrying. Even now, without any real protection from the cold, I was afraid it could be too late.

"Come with me, Amy," I said again, taking her hands and pulling her up.

"I wanna stay here," she said again, but didn't resist.

I led her away from the tree and we laboriously climbed the loose slope to the cave. With each step we took up the mountain, our feet slid half way back down through the powder. I put one arm around Amy's waist and helped her along as best I could.

At the snowmobile, I brushed off the snow and pulled the pack from the back. It took a few minutes to make it the next fifteen feet to the cave, but once there, I took the foil-coated thermal tarp from the pack and laid it inside the cave. "Crawl in here," I told Amy. She didn't respond until I lifted one of her arms over my neck and helped her stand. "You can go back to sleep after we get inside, okay?"

This promise stirred her a little, and she crawled inside and lay down on the tarp. I crawled behind her into the pitch-black interior. Sitting beside her and ducking below the low roof, I pulled off my gloves and fumbled through the pack to find the ancient chemical heat packs, opening them and shaking them to get them working, hoping they still had a little heat left.

Unzipping Amy's coat, I slid heat packs under her arms and put others against her neck, anywhere near her core where the blood ran close to the surface. Warming her too quickly, I knew, could be dangerous. Toxins had built up in the blood in her extremities that had nearly ceased to circulate, and anything that would start the cold blood moving again too quickly could shock the heart and kill her.

I unzipped my own coat and lay down, wrapping my arms around Amy and pulling the tarp around us as best I could. I was still hot and it felt good to cool down as my body heat warmed Amy. I had done everything I could now except keep Amy awake until she was out of danger.

"Okay, Amy, you have to talk to me for a minute now."

Courage, Love and the Meaning of Christmas

"Oh, Spencer. I was so cold, but I'm warm now," she said, drifting off to sleep.

"Amy, tell me about Netta," I tried.

"Oh, she's my sister. She likes you a lot."

"What else?"

"That's all. Good night. Sleep tight."

We kept talking like that until Amy's body began to warm up. I moved the heat packs from time to time. Soon chilblains set in and Amy cried and squirmed at the intense stinging, needle-like pain in her feet and finger tips. It was then that I knew she was out of danger. I stroked her hair to comfort her as the pain passed, and then she fell asleep in my arms.

My thoughts turned to Jim and Mr. Hall, still riding somewhere out in the storm. They would keep moving, at least, and the electric warmers on the handlebars would keep them from any serious danger of hypothermia, and they had each other to help. They would make it through the storm all right one way or another.

Outside our tiny snow cave, the wind howled on and the sound of snow skiffing along and dropping at the cave entrance continued through the dark night.

28 Meadows & Moonlight

I don't know when I dozed off, but I awoke in the darkness, stiff and cold on the bottom half of my body. Amy still slept, curled up next to me, breathing softly in my face.

The cave was pitch black and the sounds of wind and falling snow had ceased. I stirred, trying to get a little more comfortable, and I heard Amy's breathing pattern change as she awoke.

"Good morning, dear," she said as she began to get her bearings. "Where are we?"

"Alive and warm," I answered. "In a snow cave. It sounds like the storm's over."

We both rolled over as much as possible in our cramped quarters and slid toward the entrance, which had sealed itself off with the drifting snow that settled there. I kicked the hole bigger and we crawled outside.

The full moon hung low on the western horizon in a cloudless black sky. The air was cold but dry, and the snow-covered ground sparkled beautifully in the moonlight.

We found Grandpa's sled where I left it, buried in two feet of new snow. We brushed it off and found the windshield shattered, the engine cover cracked, and the headlight crushed.

We each grabbed one of the skis and pulled sideways until the sled was pointing almost downhill. A few tries with the ignition had the engine purring - at least that didn't seem damaged. I sat down and Amy stepped on behind me, still wrapped tight in the silver tarp. She put one arm around my waist and I hit the gas.

At first, we only inched forward through the powder, but the steep hill got us moving as loose snow tumbled alongside us.

I squeezed the throttle wide and we continued moving slowly but didn't get stuck as the weight of two people provided extra traction. The full moon supplied plenty of light to find our way down the canyon, and soon the central clearing where we had eaten lunch opened up before us. The snow here had been exposed to more wind, and the packed drifts below the spinning track provided ample traction as the long tread bit in and sent us speeding smoothly along.

Across the clearing, two snowmobile headlights appeared. One was stopped and we watched the other fly towards it, turning off at the last possible moment, and continue on for another fifty yards before it, too, slowed and stopped, bogged down in powder. By this time the first had pulled itself onto the other's trail and repeated the maneuver.

We crossed the open space with the full moon illuminating our way and pulled up alongside a sled just as it came to a slow halt.

"Daddy!" Amy yelled, jumping off the sled and toward her father.

"Oh, Amy!" he sobbed, relief gushing freely from his tired eyes. He was soaked through from having driven, no doubt, all through the storm, from digging his and Jim's snowmobiles out of the powder again and again.

Amy jumped into his arms. "Relax, Daddy," she whispered, "I'm fine. Spencer took good care of me."

Mr. Hill turned toward me, still clinging tightly to his daughter, and shook my hand heartily. "Thank you, Spencer," he said, his voice low and husky. "Thank you." He didn't let go of my hand, but pulled me toward him and hugged me, too. I hugged him back, sandwiching Amy between us.

Jim pulled up then and Amy ran through the deep snow to hug him, too. "Jimmy! You're soaked! What are you doing outside on a night like this?" she scolded.

Courage, Love and the Meaning of Christmas

"You jus' won't stay out o' trouble, will ya, girl?" he chided back.

"Ya done good, boy," he said, turning to me. He stepped over to me through the snow and shook my hand firmly, then glanced down at the crumpled front end of my sled.

"I told ya you couldn't handle this machine."

We both laughed and shook hands even harder through our thick gloves.

29 Nearby

A few cars still stood idling in the parking lot and I drove home alone after Jim helped me load my damaged sled into the truck. Someone offered to give me a ride back to town, but I told him I would be fine. Everyone there was full of handshakes and pats on the back once they heard the story. Many of them had spent hours searching in the storm before giving up or stopping for a break to warm up.

The ride home felt long and relaxing. I turned the heater on high once the engine had warmed up and drove home in silence.

I walked in the front door at Grandma's and picked up the phone first thing. Amy and Mr. Hall would already be home, but I called Andrea and told her everyone was safe.

"Would you make sure everyone knows as soon as they wake up?" I asked.

"Oh, I'm certain half the town's still up. Thanks for checking in," she said.

I set the phone down and turned to find Grandma asleep on the couch, then went to my room and changed into dry clothes before waking her.

"Grandma," I said, shaking her gently. "Grandma, I'm home. Everyone's okay."

She woke up slowly, then started when she remembered what had happened.

"Everyone's okay," I repeated.

She hugged me then and sobbed for a moment. "Oh, Spencer, I'm so glad," she said. "I was so worried."

"Ya know something, Grandma?" I said. "I felt like Grandpa was right there with me. I was never really afraid."

"I felt the same thing," she agreed. "And it felt so good, but I was afraid he had come to take you away with him."

"I think he's been around for a while, Grandma. Maybe he's always nearby."

"Maybe he is, Spencer, maybe he is."

I walked Grandma up to her room and then crawled into my own bed. I thought I wouldn't sleep for a long time. I meant to stay awake and review in my mind all the details of the night's exciting events. I fell asleep the moment my head touched the pillow.

30 Involved

I awoke when a hand touched my shoulder. I had been dreaming about the old days, living here as a child, and the heavy quilts draped over my body reminded me of every other morning I had ever woken up here. Must be time to get up and squeeze some fresh cow juice for Grandma. Funny the creaking floorboards in the hallway didn't wake me up already.

I began to roll over and found my muscles stiff and sore. The illusion vanished and I began to remember last night's ride. I turned to find Annetta sitting on the edge of my bed. My bleary eyes couldn't make out the time on the clock radio across the room, but I knew it was early since the sky hadn't quite grown light outside the window.

"Good morning, Spencer," she said. "How does our hero feel today?"

I sat up and stretched slowly, the aches multiplying as I moved. "Never better."

Before I could finish my stretch, Netta threw her arms around my neck and chest and hugged me tight. Her hands felt warm against my back, and her hair fell softly against my face. My sore arms reached around her waist and held her body tight against me.

"I did a lot of thinking last night," she said with her face still buried in my shoulder. "You've been so brave and I've been such a coward."

"What are you talking about?" I asked. "You've been wonderf…."

Netta pulled away enough to press her finger against my lips. "Shhh," she said. "Let me finish." I kissed her finger and listened. "I've been a coward, and you were right. I realized last night that if I never saw you again, I would regret not…not being honest with you, for the rest of my life. And I realized that no matter what, I'm already too attached to you to pretend I'm not."

She paused, looked down, then into my eyes.

"Honest about what?" I asked.

Courage, Love and the Meaning of Christmas

"Honest about what I really want."

"And what is that?"

"I…" she began, but couldn't finish and she looked away. "I want…" she began again, but once again looked away. Finally she looked up again with her strong, confident gaze. She slid a hand across my cheek and past my ear, then leaned forward and kissed me. The first kiss was long and slow. Her silky-smooth lips pressed against mine as the tip of her tongue softly traced my upper lip. I pulled her close and her slender waist fit perfectly in my arms, her body warm and soft against me.

Annetta's hand slid behind my head, her fingers running through my hair, and she kissed the corner of my mouth, my cheek, ear and neck with soft, wet kisses. When she finally pulled away, there was a new look in her sparkling green eyes. Love. Openness. Vulnerability.

"I'm crazy about you, Spencer Cook," she whispered with her face just inches from mine, "and I want…to get involved. Sort of."

"What do you mean, 'sort of'?" I asked.

Netta sat up a bit straighter and I lay back on the bed.

"Well…" she thought out loud, then looked down at me and said, "scoot over." I did and she lay down next to me on the quilts. She leaned against me and rested one arm on my chest. "You'd never know it, Spencer," she explained, "but everyone else does. I'm a very stubborn person. Once I make up my mind, it almost never changes.

"I'm also very practical. I'm not a big risk taker – at least when it comes to my heart. I used to be more careless – or care free – but it takes too long to pick up the pieces afterward, so I decided to change. And I did, and I stuck to it. I had dozens of friends and a few boyfriends who accused me of always keeping my distance, which was true. That's the way I wanted it.

"And then along comes this guy," Netta paused to lean over and kiss me again, "who makes me want to reconsider. I resist, of course, because it's so ridiculous. I'm leaving the country in a few weeks! Why on earth would I begin something and then just leave it?

"And then," she continued, "in just a *few days* – that part still makes me kind of mad…" Netta laughed and kissed me again, this time another long, soft one, after which she lay down against my chest, her head on the pillow with her mouth near my ear. "…he makes me change my mind and want to give it a shot.

"I'm not saying I was wrong," Netta clarified, "I wasn't. But for now… Spencer," she almost whispered, her voice now as soft as her lips, "you stir feelings inside me that I had entirely forgotten about. I haven't felt this way since I was a little girl. I like it…and I think that maybe… maybe it will be worth it this time. Maybe after I pick up the pieces, I'll find more of myself than I had before."

So that's what 'sort of getting involved' means, I thought. Going for it for now, but still breaking up and picking up the pieces later. Unlike Annetta, I could not consider future costs. I could not think beyond this exact moment in time. I would work out the details later. I scratched her back softly and kissed her cheek and ear. I closed my eyes to relax and fully enjoy this dream coming true…and instantly fell back asleep.

In my dream, I stand on a wind-swept granite outcropping. The snow-covered earth and cloud-ridden sky spreads out far below me.

Netta sits on another ridge a few hundred feet away, her back to a large rock and arms wrapped around her knees for warmth.

I shout and wave my arms to get her attention, and finally she looks my way.

She stares at me in silence for a few moments, then shouts something back; but the howling wind sweeps her words away, tumbling them down the rocky slopes until they shatter into a thousand tiny fragments and cease to exist.

She turns her face back toward the valleys below and will not look at me again.

I feel lost and alone.

31 Ninety & Nine

Annetta and I walked into the chapel hand in hand. The meeting had begun twenty minutes ago and the choir sang the final verse of *Oh, Holy Night.* As we sat down on the back row, a few heads turned and then whispered to each other. The whispering stopped as the bishop nodded and Mr. Hall stood and made his way to the pulpit. He rested his hands on either side and took a deep breath.

"I am," he began, then continued after a brief pause, "extremely, eternally, unforgettably grateful to God and everyone in this room for your assistance and prayers in the safe return of my daughter Amy early this morning.

"If it had been any of you lost in the storm, I still would have stayed out searching all night long with everyone else. But Amy…" Mr. Hall shook his head and took a few deep breaths to get his emotions under control. "Thank you," he finally said. "Thank you all." He caught my eye as he walked back to his seat and clasped his hands tightly together momentarily, holding them near his chin as sincere, overwhelming gratitude poured from his eyes.

All eyes then turned to Amy who reluctantly walked to the stand. "I'm very happy to be here today," she began, then paused, as if expecting a laugh. "And I'm sorry for all the trouble and worry I caused you all."

A few heads in the congregation shook as if to say 'No, no trouble; don't you worry about it.'

"And nobody has to get me anything for Christmas this year, or ever, because last night you got me something that will last for the rest of my life." Amy paused again. "My *life*," she prompted, and a few murmured chuckles sounded around the room.

"I don't know what else to say except thank you; thank you all so much for looking for me, and I'll never forget it, and I love you so much."

Amy craned her neck to find me in the crowd as she made her way back to her seat, then winked and blew me a kiss.

I suddenly found everyone's eyes turned expectantly toward me. I didn't know what I would say to this crowd; I didn't feel comfortable trying to explain that my dead Grandpa had told me to go and shown me where to find Amy, so I just shook my head to decline the implied invitation to speak.

The bishop then stood at the pulpit and looked over the congregation. "Last night," he began, "and this morning, we witnessed a miracle. Now you may think it was no miracle, that it was nothing more than a lot of hard work and determination and maybe a little luck that brought Amy back to us. But miracles most often come through people the Lord puts in the right place at the right time, and it's not always easy for those people to accomplish such miracles.

"And the truth is, we're surrounded continually, every day of our lives, by opportunities to participate in miracles. People all around need a helping hand, or a sympathetic ear, or just some company to pass the time. The question is whether or not we will step up and accept the invitation, and step out of our comfort zone, and reach out to one another.

"Love. Love is the greatest miracle of all. To think that a mere feeling could prompt us to suffer, unflinchingly, uncomplaining, through the worst conditions imaginable, in order to relieve the suffering of others.

"In good times, love fills us with joy and rejoicing. In hard times, love lends us the courage to carry on. In the darkest of dark times, in the midst of anguish and misery, when all hope is stripped away and nothing good seems to remain, it leaves us with no other option - if we cling to love - but to endure, to persevere, and stay the course.

"Of course especially at this time of year, we think of our Savior – not only His birth, but what made that birth so significant – His life, His teachings, and above all else, His suffering in Gethsemane and on the cross.

"I used to think that although it was certainly agonizingly painful for Him, that perhaps it was also relatively easy, He being a God. I don't believe that anymore.

"Now I believe it was the most difficult act anyone has ever accomplished, by far. I think it taxed even Him to His divine limits. I think it took tremendous amounts of strength and courage and love – far more than I can begin to comprehend.

"And yet He endured. He saved us all, and why? Because He loves us. Because He loves us, He willingly accepted the weight of the world, endured the price of every sin ever to be committed, all to rescue us from a price we could not pay ourselves, and save us from a terrible prison we could never otherwise escape."

The incomprehensibly sweet and powerful Holy Spirit flooded into the room while the bishop spoke and confirmed his words, carrying their meaning deep into our hearts and softening any hardness we carried there, opening our hearts and making us willing to allow just a little more love to enter in and flow out.

The bishop looked around the room, making eye contact with many faces, most of their eyes already brimming with tears. "Until this morning," he confided, "I thought I understood the Meaning of Christmas. I thought Christmas simply meant the celebration of the birth of our Lord and Savior, and a beautiful time in which we stop thinking mostly about ourselves and turn outward instead with warm greetings and a few gifts.

"But now I understand that Christmas means much more than just that. When Jesus commanded his followers to come, follow Him, He didn't mean to bake fruitcake and decorate trees, though that's all fine and good. He meant to love, to truly reach out and *love* everyone, even when it's hard, even when it's uncomfortable and inconvenient, even at great personal risk and when time seems to be running out and the

Courage, Love and the Meaning of Christmas

chance of success seems to be dimming.

"That is exactly what you did last night. God bless you all for your love. For your dedication. For your sacrifice. For your discipleship.

"My brothers and sisters, *that* is the true Meaning of Christmas. That we not only show our love to family and friends, but that we leave the comfort of our warm homes and comfort zones and go out into the storm to rescue the poor, the needy, the lonely, the lost, and the cold.

"We are told that the angels gathered together and sang hallelujahs on that night two thousand years ago when Jesus was born, because He had at long last come to fulfill the promise and save us all. Brothers and sisters, I believe you regularly make those angels sing hallelujahs all over again. God bless you all."

32 Over & Only Just Begun

When the service ended, small crowds gathered around Amy and I, anxious to hear the story of last night's adventure first hand. I wasn't quite comfortable being such a center of attention, but complied anyway.

A few people noticed that Amy's and my versions of the story differed somewhat. When Amy accused me of downplaying my part in the events, I jokingly reminded her that she had been delirious and her mind must have exaggerated the facts.

The Halls invited Grandma and me over for Sunday dinner after church. "I don't know how to thank you, Spencer," Mr. Hall kept saying. "Then don't worry about it," I'd answer; "I understand. I don't need any thanks."

"Hey, Netta," Amy teased, "wanna hear what *really* happened inside that cozy little snow cave?"

I sat in the living room while Netta went upstairs to change. Amy walked in and sat sideways on the couch next to me. "I haven't seen my sister this happy since before our mom got sick," she announced with satisfaction.

"Really?" I asked, wondering why Netta never told me anything about their mother. "What does she have?"

"She didn't tell you?" Amy asked, raising an eyebrow in surprise. "I shouldn't be shocked to hear that. She doesn't like to talk about it even though it's been ten years."

"Ten years since she got sick?"

"No," Amy answered nonchalantly. "Ten years since she died."

"What?!" I blurted out, feeling shocked at the abrupt revelation. "I had no idea. I'm sorry to hear that."

"Hey," Amy said, waving it off, "these things happen."

"Really?" I asked incredulously. "Is it that easy for you now?"

"It's the past," Amy explained. "I miss her sometimes, sure, but getting all depressed about it won't bring her back."

I stared at Amy in admiration of her ability to let go and move on. "What did she have?" I asked.

"She caught some kind of heart worm when we lived in Brazil. By the time the doctors figured out what was making her sick, it was too late to treat it."

"I can't imagine how devastating that would be," I admitted.

"We moved to Hawaii after that, and had a few more years together, but even then, Netta was in total denial the whole time. She got mad or left the house whenever Mom took her medication, and she almost didn't come to the hospital to finally say goodbye."

"Wow. And this is happiest you've seen her since then?"

"You," Amy said, reaching over to touch my arm, "broke through the impenetrable wall. She's never let anyone else really get to her heart since she was twelve years old. But I shouldn't be surprised."

"I know," I agreed. "That sounds rough."

"No, not that!" Amy objected. "I mean I'm not surprised that *you* broke through her walls."

"Why's that?" I asked, curious and eager for whatever compliment I hoped would follow.

"Because my dear sister Annetta never outgrew her fairy tale expectations. Despite her distant and cold exterior, she still believes that the meaning of life is to live in a continual state of bliss. So when along comes the dashing, charming, confident Spencer Cook, who not only swears his undying devotion to her, but rides into the storm to slay the dragon; well, how could she resist? Her sweetest dreams have all come true and nothing bad can ever happen again as she and her doting Prince Charming live happily ever after."

I expected Amy's explanation to make me feel good, but by the time she finished, I felt a bit uncomfortable instead. "I don't know if I can promise that."

"Of course you can't," Amy agreed. "Life is *not* bliss. It's hard! It's downright brutal sometimes."

"But if you accept that," I said thoughtfully, "then...."

"Then you get over it," Amy interrupted. "You let go and get on with living."

"And it's not *all* hard," I continued.

"No, not at all!" Amy agreed enthusiastically, sitting up straighter as her eyes lit up. "It's so beautiful! Even when things are hard, life is still so beautiful!"

"So what happens to Annetta when things don't turn out perfectly?" I asked, still a little worried about the daunting task I had unwittingly taken on.

"Oh, I wouldn't worry too much about that," Amy reassured me. "She already knows it can't last. And this time she's the one leaving, so she won't feel abandoned and betrayed."

Amy's reassurance didn't exactly reassure me. What did she mean, exactly, that this couldn't last? Had everything really already been decided? But before I could formulate and ask the question, Netta came downstairs and called us to dinner.

Once we had eaten, my full stomach and the lack of sleep started catching up to me, and I could hardly keep my eyes open. As the conversation around the table continued, I was escorted to the living room couch and given a blanket. "It's the least we can do," everyone kept saying. I was too drowsy to argue.

When I woke up, Grandma had gone home and everyone else was just settling down for a nap. Annetta had already curled up with a pillow and blanket on the floor next to the couch. Her eyes were closed and she seemed to be asleep. Isn't life ironic, I thought. I finally find just what I want, and I can only keep it for another week.

I began reviewing my options. We could write and I could hope someday we'd be together again and wait and see what came of it. I could go back to school and try to replace her, maybe even put her out of my mind until we could see each other again. Neither option sounded very good. I could try to convince her to come back sooner than three years. I could move to France myself. Neither of these options sounded very likely to happen right away. I could visit her in France, but then I'd have to come home and find myself in the exact same situation. Plans like that would take more time to develop. I'd just have to wait and let life play itself out.

Annetta's eyes opened and she looked up at me. "Whatcha thinkin' about?"

"You," I answered.

Annetta frowned at this. "You don't look too happy. Is something wrong?"

"No," I answered, "but it will be in about a week."

Her frown faded and she nodded empathetically. "I'll miss you, too."

"So what happens then?"

"Well," she answered, "life goes on."

I thought about that for a moment. "And what does that mean, exactly?"

"It means you go back to school and I go to France," she answered. "You've already paid tuition and I already have a plane ticket."

"I see," I said, but I didn't see at all. How could this girl start out so determined not to get involved in a short-term relationship so suddenly flip to the opposite extreme and become so determined to get serious for a week and then end it that abruptly? Had I missed something? Had I misunderstood her intentions? My mind was still a bit groggy from sleep and my hazy thoughts all ran together. I gave it one more chance. "And then what?"

"Then we write and go on with our lives. You have to trust life to work out. I've never lived in France, so I don't know what to expect. I'll look for a job and go from there. And you, you have school to finish. You must have lots of friends, and I'm sure all the girls will be dying to go out with you."

So it was true. She didn't plan to see me again and was telling me to get on with my life, and without her. "And you're okay with that?" I asked.

"It helps a lot that I'm going to France, I think. The two weeks here without you will be lonely, but I'll be so excited to explore the cities and beaches and practice my French, that I'm sure I'll get by all right."

At least I wouldn't have to worry about her being okay. I turned my face the other way, into the couch cushions. I didn't feel like looking at her anymore.

"So what about you?" she asked. "Do you have any exciting classes? Are you looking forward to going back to school?"

I thought about what I had to look forward to. Classes would be okay, but nothing I'd call exciting. For a moment, I remembered Julie, her bright blue eyes, her smile, her face that was even more beautiful than Netta's. Then I remembered the way her eyes lit up when she and Ski had gone off together after finals. No, nothing to look forward to there, either. At least I had the canyons full of snow and my cross-country skis.

"Hey, I know," Annetta continued, "you could take a French class!"

Maybe she had known to plan for this goodbye all along, but I hadn't. It never occurred to me that she could let go so easily. Now she was trying to lighten things up, to cheer me up, but I didn't feel like cheering up.

When I didn't answer, Annetta sat up and scratched my back. I guess I only had myself to blame for everything. I had made my wish, it had come true, and now I had to live with the consequences. I was the one pushing for us to get more serious all along, and when she allowed me to pull her closer, I had assumed that her feelings had changed as well. I assumed that she, like me, would start thinking about the long term.

This entire misunderstanding is my fault, I thought. *I can't blame her for anything.* I turned my face back to her. I would muster up a little courage and try to take it as well as I could. "Oui," I said. "C'est la vie."

Netta laughed at this and hugged me. I hugged her back half-heartedly. It made me feel a little better.

"You look hammered," she said. "Do you want me to take you home?"

"Yeah, I guess that sounds good," I answered, trying to decide whether or not I'd rather be alone.

I folded the blanket and set it on the couch, then put my shoes back on. My shirt was wrinkled and my face probably still carried the red impressions from the couch fabric. We walked out to the car and the bright sunlight made me squint.

A perfect winter day shone all around us, but all I could think about on the drive home was how much longer it would take for Spring to arrive. Then I would finally be able to hike comfortably in the hills. I could sit in the new, tall mountain grasses and flowers and watch the wind dance in patterns over them without growing cold. I could spend entire days lying on my back there, staring up at the blue, blue sky as sunlight filtered through high leaves swaying gently in the breeze. Maybe then I would feel better. Maybe then I could forget all about Annetta and this roller coaster Christmas vacation.

Grandma opened the front door and invited Annetta in before she could drop me off. Netta held my hand as we walked up the steps and into the living room. Grandma disappeared into the kitchen and emerged with two pieces of pumpkin pie dabbed with whipped cream.

"I came home and just couldn't sit still," she told us excitedly. "Usually when I come home to the empty house, it feels so big and empty. But today," she searched for the right word, "today felt different. I came home and was just so happy. It's as if a shadow has been lifted from me."

Annetta squeezed my hand extra hard. I knew what she meant. Maybe things had changed permanently for Grandma.

"Maybe it's knowing that Spencer and Amy are safe," Grandma continued. "Or seeing you two so happy together. Or knowing that tomorrow night all my children and grandchildren will begin to arrive."

Grandma's homemade pumpkin pie is my favorite food in the world. I ate slowly, savoring each bite. This also kept me from having to say much. Inside, I was torn between loving Annetta and wanting to back off and protect my heart. Courage was a different matter when I thought she was only playing it safe. If I had known all along that the relationship just didn't mean that much to her or that she didn't plan to keep it once we both moved away, I would have been wiser and never would have pressed for more involvement.

"You still look awfully tired," Annetta said. "Do you want to go upstairs and get more sleep?"

"Yeah, maybe I should," I answered.

Annetta walked me up to my room where she gave me a tight squeeze and a soft kiss. "Sweet dreams, Spencer," she said. "I get off tomorrow at four."

"Wanna drop by and meet my family?" I asked. I would probably feel better by then anyway. Maybe I had been blowing everything out of proportion.

"Sounds great," she said, kissing me again. I held her warm body against me for a minute, then walked into my room and laid down, but couldn't sleep. I picked up the copy of Les Mis from the library and started reading. From downstairs, the happy voices of my two favorite girls floated up to my ears.

33 C'est La Vie

I read late into the night and picked up the book again as soon as I woke up the next morning. By the time I got up and showered at three thirty in the afternoon, I had read enough to learn that life is not fair. It had never occurred to me that I expected it to be.

Netta would show up soon, and I decided to discuss the idea with her. Maybe that would help me feel better about the situation between us. I could at least tell her some of my thoughts and we could reach a better understanding. Maybe she'd even change her perspective a bit and allow for the possibility of a more lasting relationship, even if it meant carrying that on long distance.

At four o'clock I checked outside to see if Annetta had come yet and realized that she would just be getting off work. I suddenly missed having cell service so I could at least send her a text. "See you soon!" I'd write, and she would reply by commenting on how she couldn't wait.

I picked up the book again and read on. I was entirely immersed in the story until the doorbell rang three chapters later. I threw the book on my bed and ran downstairs. I was in a much better mood than yesterday and was anxious again to see Annetta.

When I reached the stairs, I noticed how much time had passed. The shadows stretched all along the living room floor as my family carried bags of clothes and food inside from the car.

"Spencer!" cried my youngest sister, dropping her gym bag in the doorway and running to meet me on the stairs. Diane had just started kindergarten this fall.

"Hey, baby sister!" I laughed, picking her up and swinging her around.

"I'm not a baby!" she objected. "I'm five."

I gave her a tight squeeze and she squeezed back as hard as she could in the game we called 'squeeze your air out.'

"Diane!" Alisha yelled. "Get your bag out of the way!" Alisha was twelve and was just making her way through the front door with four full duffel bags of clothes and toys for the week away from home.

"Spencer!" she said when she saw me, her tone changing instantly. She set her things down near the couch and walked over for her hug. "Why didn't you come home first?" she asked, looking puzzled and like she had missed me.

"Well," I told her, "I knew there wouldn't be room for me in the car with all your stuff anyway. Also, there was this girl here I wanted to meet."

"A girl? Woo-woo," she teased. "Spencer has a girlfriend," she added in a sing-song voice.

"You do?" Diane asked. "Who is she?"

"Her name's Annetta," I answered. "And you can meet her soon when she comes over." I glanced up at the grandfather clock. Five thirty. I wondered what was taking her so long. Maybe she had to stay home for dinner.

Mom and Dad came in next, hugging me or shaking my hand and wishing me Merry Christmas.

"So what have you done with yourself since you've been up here?" Dad asked.

"Oh, I've done some reading and made a few friends. Mostly just relaxed after a tough semester."

"I see," Dad said in his way that meant he wondered if I could have used my time more productively.

"And that's exactly what he plans to keep doing, too," Mom chimed in protectively, "so don't you say a thing about it."

"Will you be coming home with us this weekend?" Dad asked.

"I think I'll be staying here till school starts, actually," I answered.

"That sounds great," Mom said. "You can keep Grandma company and help her with…."

A sudden stern look from Dad stopped the rest of her sentence. Mom smiled at both of us and pretended there wasn't anything else to say.

Grandma announced then that dinner was almost ready and she could use some help setting the table. "Should we set a place for Annetta?" she asked me.

I wished I knew. I wished I could message her and ask. I would write, "What's up? You okay?" and she would reply and I would quit worrying. I could always phone, but I didn't want half the town listening in to our private conversation, which is probably why she hadn't called, either.

"Looks like she's not coming," I answered. "Maybe she'll drop by later."

At ten o'clock, Netta still hadn't shown up. I had long since given up hope of seeing her tonight and had decided to just play it cool for the rest of vacation. More cousins would be here tomorrow and I'd have plenty of catching up and things to keep my mind off her. I could always change my mind later, but for now, I didn't want any more disappointment.

"Hey Spencer," Alisha said as we sat around playing scrabble, "how about a snowmobile ride tomorrow?"

"I'm afraid we won't be riding the snowmobile for a few days at least."

"Why not?" she asked, with everyone else looking curiously on.

"I sort of wrecked it."

"You what?!" Dad and Alisha said simultaneously.

"I hit a big drift and crunched up the front end. It still runs, but I should get it fixed first. It's probably gonna cost a couple hundred dollars."

Courage, Love and the Meaning of Christmas

"Before anyone gets too upset," Grandma interrupted, "you should know that Spencer saved a young woman's life."

Dad's eyebrows raised, surprised, as Alisha complained, "Yeah, but did you have to wreck the snowmobile?"

"Yeah," I answered. "I had to."

"What's all this about saving someone's life?" Dad asked.

"Oh," I answered, "this girl got stuck in a storm so I went and got her."

"Why did you have to wreck the snowmobile?" Alisha asked again.

"Cause there was a big drift in the way."

"Why couldn't you just go around?"

"Cause I had to go through it."

"Uh, uh! You could have gone around it instead!"

"But then we would have been too cold."

"Was it your girlfriend?" Diane asked.

"No," I answered. "It was her sister. But she's not my girlfriend, anyway."

Grandma looked surprised. She told everyone the story of the storm and the snow cave. "I'm proud of you, Spencer," Dad said. "How about if I help you pay to repair it?"

"Thanks, Dad," I said. "That's really nice of you."

"That's cool," Alisha said, no longer complaining, then sat up straighter. "I wanna see it."

We all put on our coats and walked out to the barn where I searched through the truck's glove box for a flashlight.

"Looks alright to me," Dad said as I stepped down with the flashlight. It felt nice to have Dad go easy on me for once and I appreciated it. I turned on the light and shone it on the snowmobile to show the damage, but…there was none. The windshield stood straight and unbroken atop the smooth engine cover and uncracked headlight. My mouth dropped open in surprise.

"Well…that was a pretty good story," Dad said after a moment's pause. "You sure had us going along with it."

Alisha looked at me funny, wondering why Grandma and I had made up such a strange story. "So can we go for a ride tomorrow?" she asked.

"Yeah, sure," I answered, wondering who could have fixed the sled. I ran my fingers under the cowling and found half a dozen washers to correct the spacing and make the cover fit straight where the crash had bent the frame.

The others walked back inside but I stayed in the barn, sitting on the snowmobile for a while, holding the familiar handlebars and sorting out my thoughts and feelings. Why hadn't Annetta come or even called? Could she have been the one to fix the sled? No, the parts must have been picked up in Evanston, and if she worked till four, she wouldn't have had time to pick them up and do the repair. Maybe she just got busy—but with what?

Oh, well, life's not fair, I reminded myself. I jumped out of the truck bed and walked out of the barn. The stars shone brightly in the black winter sky. The moon wasn't up yet and I decided to go for a walk in the dark. I set out between the cornstalks still standing straight and dry. Snow crunched below my feet as I walked, and nature worked its magic on me, getting inside and calming me again, soothing away most of the pain of disappointment for the moment.

I kept walking for what must have been half an hour. By then the cold had worked its way into my toes and face. The moon was just inching over the horizon, turning the sky light and erasing the dimmest stars. I turned around and headed home. The house lights were all off when I arrived and I slipped quietly upstairs to my room and fell asleep.

34 Starting Fresh

Alisha and Diane barged into my room early the next morning to wake me up for breakfast.

"Hurry!" Diane said as I gulped down the lumpy oatmeal they had fixed me.

We drove to the mountain parking lot, I backed the truck up to the snow pile, and we dragged the sled out of the back. I started the engine to let it warm up while we put on our snow gear, then we all crowded onto the seat and rode away.

We drove to the clearing and I let each sister take a turn driving around by herself while I chatted with the other and caught up on school and what books they were reading and which of their friends were being nice and which ones weren't.

The clearing felt empty and big with only one snowmobile in it, but I liked it this way. All the former tracks had been completely erased. Everything had turned fresh, had become a brand-new start, as easy as that. *I can do that*, I told myself, thinking about Annetta. *I can just start*

Courage, Love and the Meaning of Christmas

over. Now that I knew the rules, the game would work out better.

Once Alisha and Diane had both taken a few turns driving, I checked the gas tank and found it nearly empty. "That's gonna be it for today," I told the girls.

They each took short turns driving us back to the truck and we loaded it up. It was two o'clock when we reached town again and pulled off the highway near Becca's.

"Let's stop for hot chocolate," Alisha suggested.

"We're almost home," I said. "We can get some there."

"Please!" Diane begged. "I'm *so* cold!"

The five-year-old was so cute with that desperate look on her face that I almost gave in, but I was starting over and didn't feel like doing it with the complication of explaining everything to Netta and my little sisters at the same time. We kept driving and I saw Annetta's car in the parking lot along with a dozen others.

"Oh," Diane said, "I was supposed to tell you Natalie stopped by last night."

"Who?" I asked.

"Nanette," Alisha corrected her.

"Annetta?" I asked.

"Yeah, that's it."

I stepped on the brake and turned the truck around.

"Where are we going?" Alisha asked.

"Do you still want hot chocolate?" I asked.

"Yes!" they both shouted happily. Knowing Annetta had come by last night after all made me want to see her again. I could cut her a little slack, but that didn't mean I was changing my plans.

"I think she likes you," Alisha said.

"Oh, yeah? Why's that?"

"'Cause I asked her why she's not your girlfriend and she didn't say anything."

"Hey! It's Spencer!" someone cried as we walked inside the diner. Half the tables were full. I had never seen the place so busy. "The hero!" said someone else at the counter. "Whatever he orders, I'm paying for it!" said a third. Everyone was in high holiday spirits. I waved and said hello to the crowd of strangers, feeling like a celebrity, and walked to a corner booth with my sisters.

Alisha and Diane both wanted to sit by me, so I scooted behind the table to the middle. "What's everyone talking about?" Alisha asked, looking confused and curious.

"Remember that story Grandma told you last night? Well it's true. And that's the girl right over there," I said, pointing to Amy who was taking an order at another table. She finished and walked over to us.

"Long time no see," she said. It had been two full days now. "What can I get you all?"

"Three hot chocolates, please," Alisha ordered.

"Large," Diane added.

"Did my brother really save your life?" Alisha asked.

"Yep, he sure did," Amy answered, smiling happily at her. "It was just like being in a movie."

I introduced the three of them and someone called Amy to ask when their food would be ready.

"Gotta run," she said. "Nice to meet you all."

Annetta walked over to our table a minute later with three mugs of hot chocolate on a tray. She had been in the kitchen and wore an apron and her hair in a ponytail. "Hi, guys," she said, setting our mugs on the table. "Diane, did you want extra whipped cream?"

"Yes!" Diane answered excitedly.

"Thanks for dropping by," Netta said.

"Well, my sisters begged till I had to give in."

"What have you been up to?" she asked.

"Oh," I answered, "life's just going on. The family's all showing up now, so we keep pretty busy there." I wanted to downplay the fact that she hadn't come till so late last night. There was no reason to make a big deal about it.

"Sorry I missed you last night," Netta added. "Where were you?"

"Just out for a walk. It's nice out there at night—so quiet and all." That should do it, make it sound like I didn't even mind, like I hadn't missed her that much, like I would be all right on my own, too. That should put her mind at ease.

She looked into my eyes then, and I knew she was trying to read what was there, just to make sure, to read me down deep inside where it's impossible to lie. "I have to get back to the kitchen before I burn something," she said. "But I get off in half an hour. Will I see you soon?"

"Sure," I answered nonchalantly. "I'll call ya sometime tonight."

I watched her walk back to the kitchen and noticed that the bounce had disappeared from her step. It's probably been a long day for her, I thought, looking around at the room full of customers.

We finished our drinks and I walked toward the cash register to pay.

"No, no, no!" said the man at the bar, shaking a finger at me. "I'm picking up your tab."

"And I'm covering the tip," said the man next to him. He slapped me on the shoulder and I thanked them both and walked outside. Ali and Di walked around to the passenger door and I was just opening mine when the diner door opened and Amy called to me.

"Hey!" she said, walking over. "What's the matter with you?"

"What do you mean?" I asked.

"I mean why are you treating my sister like that?" she said. "You're breaking her heart."

"Well I don't know how much she's told you," I said, "but if she's just planning to get on with her life as soon as I'm gone anyway, I don't know what the big deal is. Besides, she said she was coming over yesterday after work, but didn't show up till eleven o'clock. What am I supposed to think? How am I supposed to react?"

"You don't know what you're talking about!" Amy accused, shaking her head, her eyes flashing.

"I know that life's not fair and sometimes you just have to grin and bear it."

"No, life's not fair," Amy agreed, "but don't you ever let that be your fault! Netta came by late last night 'cause she didn't get off till after closing. Jim didn't show up for work and she had to cover for him. With all these crowds stopping in off the highway, she couldn't very well let me handle it alone."

"I didn't know," I said, slightly humbled. "I'm sorry."

"Please go talk to her," she said. Her eyes were half pleading, half demanding.

I nodded my head and walked back toward the door.

Amy opened my door the rest of the way. "Hey, do you two want a donut?"

"Yeah!" my sisters shouted, piling excitedly back out of the truck.

"Spencer's back!" someone yelled again as I walked back inside. "I'm paying this time!" someone else said. I couldn't help but smile. I walked into the kitchen and found Annetta tending half a dozen different items on the grill and elsewhere.

"So are you different now that you're a hero?" she asked. This time I could see by the look in her eyes that she was hurting inside.

"Please, let's not talk about that. I'm so tired of hearing about it when it was really nothing."

"What do you mean, nothing?" she asked.

"I mean I just went out there and found Amy. It was just something I did. I've thought about this enough to decide that your actions don't make you great, it's what's inside, so I'm the same person I always was and I don't know why anyone should treat me any differently now than before."

Annetta looked up from the sizzling grill. "You mean it really didn't change you at all?"

"Well maybe a little. Any experience does that, that's what you told me. But I'm pretty much the same person; so no, it didn't." I watched a tear well up in Annetta's eyes. I couldn't tell if she looked happy or sad.

"What's wrong now?" I asked. I wasn't doing a very good job of starting over. I couldn't help but care, but didn't know how to do it from a distance. And if Annetta really cared, as I was beginning to guess, then why would I want to start over anyway? If I only knew what she really thought, if I could only make sense of all the mixed, confusing messages she was sending out.

"Well if," Annetta began, "if you didn't change, then why do you act so different?"

"I'm sorry I've been so distant," I told her. "I just couldn't stay close when I realized you weren't all that serious about us."

"What do you mean?" she asked, shaking her head and speaking slowly. "What are you talking about?"

"When I didn't know why you didn't come by earlier last night—but Amy told me about that—I got thinking about everything you said about getting on with our lives and me finding other girls to date and how you'd be just fine and how we should just trust things to work out on their own. So you just didn't sound that serious about it."

Now hot tears poured freely down both of her soft cheeks. "I never meant it that way," she nearly sobbed, looking happy and sad all at the same time. "I never ever meant I wasn't serious about you!" She started to lift her arms around my neck but stopped short and backed off again. "When I said we have to trust life to work out, I meant we had to trust it to bring us back together again someday."

The truth began to sink in slowly. The little knot I had carried in my stomach since Sunday afternoon loosened a bit.

"And everything else I said," Netta explained, "was only so you wouldn't worry about me!" She stood facing me there, spatula in hand, burgers sizzling on the grill, waiting for my response.

"I guess I got everything all wrong," I said.

Netta took another step toward me. "Does this mean," she asked

Courage, Love and the Meaning of Christmas

hopefully, "that everything can be alright between us again?"

"Yeah," I said quietly. "And I'm sorry." She threw her arms around my neck then and her laughter came out like a sob. I felt her wet cheek on my neck and held her tight.

"You really haven't changed, have you?"

"How would I change?" I asked.

"I thought all that attention had gone to your head. I was beginning to think I had misjudged you all along. But I was right the first time, you really are wonderful."

I didn't know how she could possibly think so highly of me, but I wasn't about to argue. Alisha and Diane walked into the kitchen then and smiles spread slowly across their faces. "You'd better flip those burgers before they burn," I told Annetta.

"If I'm not at your place in an hour," Netta said, "call me."

"I will," I promised.

"Hey, what's the hold up in here?" Amy shouted, walking through the door. "Where are my orders?"

"Thanks," I whispered to her on my way out, touching her shoulder. She punched me back and grinned. "That's better," she said.

"Are you sure she's not your girlfriend?" Alisha asked on the ride home.

"Yeah, I guess she is," I answered.

We got home and I read another chapter of *Les Mis*. This time the lesson was different. This time I learned that no matter what happens, no matter what life throws at you, you can always find or create moments of extreme beauty by refusing to give in to the unfairness and uncertainties and day-to-day challenges of everyday life.

35 Time Flies

Annetta came by an hour later and everything went better from then on. My heart ached, At first,, for the wasted two days we could have spent together. Time is always limited and precious, but I felt acutely aware of its passing with only a week and a half left before school would begin.

We spent our time playing with our families and talking, getting to know each other as well as possible and just enjoying each other's company. I poured through Annetta's photo albums and we spent a little time reading in the library together. We rarely got more than a few pages into whatever we were reading, though, before something sparked an idea that got us talking until the library closed or she had to go to work.

"Do you like reading fiction or non-fiction best?" Annetta asked me one afternoon.

"I never really thought about it," I answered. "Why? What about you?"

"It depends," she said. "I like whatever makes me excited about things I could do with my life."

"Like what?"

"Like going new places and trying new things," she said. "Non-fiction's best for that. It sounds so easy when you're just reading along; it's inspiring. And fiction's best, if it's good, to get away from all the serious things in life, and envision something even better than reality. I get all caught up in some imaginary world and then I get all relaxed and ready to take off running again."

"And which do you want most now?"

"Now I'm torn. I'd love to be climbing a volcano in Hawaii with you right now, but since I can't, I'm content to keep on reading and forget about the snow outside for a while."

Sometimes I'd go to Becca's with her and help serve the crowd of people driving by on the highway on their way to visit relatives for the holidays. I had never realized how interesting total strangers could be.

"That's the best part of the job," Annetta told me.

The next time I saw Jim there, I put two and two together and realized he had skipped work Monday to drive to Evanston and then fix Grandpa's snowmobile and thanked him for it. He denied knowing anything about it, but I knew it was him. "If you don't want me to say anything about it, I won't," I promised, "but I really appreciate that. You're a good man." He gave me a slight nod and went on with his work.

Once all my cousins arrived, we drove into the hills and brought back a Christmas tree for the house. The family spent Christmas Eve together reading the Christmas story in Luke and singing around the old piano.

Christmas morning came early with young cousins too excited to sleep running through the large house as soon as the regulation don't-wake-anyone-up-until-seven-o'clock had passed.

The most notable gift was the computer that Dad and Mom gave Grandma. "Now we can all keep in touch easily," Mom said. "It's all

Courage, Love and the Meaning of Christmas

set up for Facebook and e-mail and video chat, and the whole family's connections are already programmed in."

"I don't know," Grandma said, "this is all so new for me."

"Ah, it's easy," Dad said. "And if you have any questions, Spencer will be around to help or you can call us."

Grandma nodded her head.

"You're going to love it once you get used to it," Mom added. "And we'll all love hearing from you more often."

"I don't mean to be a party pooper," I began, "but how are we gonna connect this to the internet?" With only antiquated phone lines, and no regular cable or hundred-gigabit-fiberoptic lines within fifty miles, the only apparent option was dial-up, and I smiled when I thought of the town party line filled with static and beeping of an old modem connection.

"A satellite dish is scheduled to be installed tomorrow," Dad explained, "and we'll connect to it with this." He reached behind the couch and lifted a simple brown cardboard box with a modem in it.

I took it from him and opened the box, then instantly noticed a minor problem. "This is just a cable modem," I pointed out. "It doesn't have wireless, so we'll need to get a wireless router, too, so we can connect our other devices."

"Actually," Dad countered, "we already took that into consideration and decided against it. This is the only chance we ever get to fully unplug, and we don't want the kids staring at their screens all day and night and missing out on one another."

"Good idea," I nodded in agreement.

Grandma gave me a framed watercolor she had painted over the summer of green mountain meadows and beautiful pastel wildflowers, and she surprised me with her succinct ability to summarize the complex idea I had struggled so long to understand – in one corner of the painting she wrote: "The Meaning of Life is to live."

Amy wrote a beautiful poem about falling snow and asked me to critique it. I taught her a few tricks about imagery and rhythm that I picked up in school and her revisions showed real promise as a writer. "Ever think of becoming an English major?"

"Should I?" she asked.

"Just keep it in mind for now," I told her.

Winter
asks us to change
our perspective.

It offers gifts
most won't receive,
But continues
to show us our breath,
to heave and sigh and
Send the sky falling,
Draping a sparkling blanket of white
Over the slumbering earth.

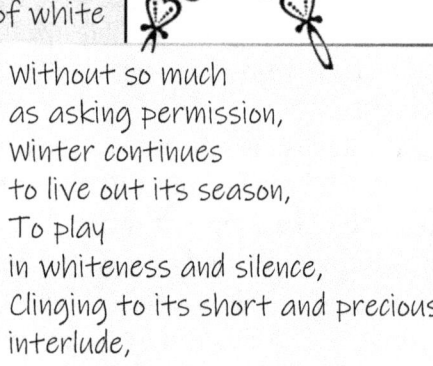

Without so much
as asking permission,
Winter continues
to live out its season,
To play
in whiteness and silence,
Clinging to its short and precious
interlude,
Tenacious and silent as icicles.

Winter is not death and cold,
Not waiting for life, for the future.
Winter is not hunger and pain,
Not saving dreams for the morning.
Winter is beauty, wake up and see!
Winter harvests individuality.

Compare any snowflakes
to find the warm truth:
Winter teaches how to change,
Flake by flake by flake
Until the world is white.

Winter makes the spring grow green,
Makes the heart grow warm.

Outside your window
Winter is falling

And melting

On outstretched, eager
Children's tongues.

36 Enduring Questions

The remaining days of Christmas vacation passed by quickly. Most of my relatives went home but my mom and little sisters decided to stay till New Year's. I divided my time between my family, the Hall's, and Becca's when Netta had to work. We rode snowmobiles, took the kids to the hot springs, and stayed up late talking, snuggling and reading together.

Two unsettling questions plagued me when I found myself alone or the distractions faded at the end of each day. First, what would happen when I went back to school?

I felt like a completely different person than before. I no longer felt shy and self-conscious. Would I carry this change back with me or quickly revert to my old ways? Had I truly changed, or was it just being around Netta that made me feel so different?

"What are you thinking about?" Netta asked one night as she sat with my arms wrapped around her staring at the glowing embers in her living room fireplace.

"Oh," I said, "nothing."

Annetta twisted around to look me in the eyes momentarily. "Nothing what?"

"Um," I began again, "remember when I told you that I used to be really shy and stuff?" She nodded. "Well…the truth is…that was about two weeks ago."

Netta twisted around again and gave me a surprised look. "Whatever!" she said incredulously.

"I'm serious," I affirmed, "and what I was thinking about just now is whether I've really changed, or if I'll revert the moment I'm away from you."

Netta leaned back against me and pulled my arms more tightly around her. "So it's a question of conversion," she observed. "Are you merely influenced by your circumstances, or has a deep and permanent change occurred."

I didn't know. How could I? Did the fact that I kept asking this question mean that I hadn't completely changed? Certainly I hadn't conquered all my insecurities yet, but it seemed like a good start. This new me felt effortless and natural, and memories of my old feelings had already grown hazy. The change felt deep even if not complete. "If it's deep, does that make it permanent?" I asked.

"Yes," she answered as if nothing could be more obvious.

Second, what would happen when I went back to school? What would become of my relationship with Netta? We could call and e-mail and video chat and follow each other on Facebook and Instagram, but would that feel the same? And what did our relationship mean, exactly, anyway? Would the remaining few days give us enough time to figure that out?

I didn't know, and the only way I knew to find out was to wait and see.

"So, Spencer," Annetta asked me over dinner at the Hall's one night, "have you figured out the meaning of life yet?"

"I think so," I said. Amy smiled and put down her fork. Mr. Hall raised an eyebrow.

"Essentially, 'meaning' is the feeling of satisfaction you experience from participating purposefully in life," I explained.

"I thought the meaning of life was supposed to tell you how to get that satisfaction," Amy said.

"Probably a lot of people are looking for that kind of answer," I continued. "But it's different for everyone, see? And it changes from day to day. Because we have all these different talents and needs to fill, so what provides meaning one day might not work as well the next week."

"So the meaning of life is just to participate in life?"

"I'd call that the *purpose* of life," I clarified. "Or *a* purpose. And meaning is what you get when you do."

"What do you mean, 'a' purpose?"

"I mean there are lots of perspectives to tell you the purpose of life. Like at school, the purpose is to learn or develop critical thinking skills or get trained on how to earn a living.

"If you're talking about religion, then the purpose is to have faith and become enlightened and converted and love your enemies and make the world a better place, even it's just by changing yourself for the better.

"If it's a weekend, then maybe the purpose of life – the way to have a satisfying, meaningful experience – is to take a memorable road trip to somewhere beautiful with good friends.

"So 'participating purposefully in life' tells you to get out there and get busy, but doesn't tell you exactly how. You have to kind of figure that out for yourself."

"Interesting," said Mr. Hall.

The next afternoon, when business slowed down at Becca's, Amy joined me in the booth where I sat reading.

"You've ruined my life," she said with a frustrated smile.

"I did?" I asked, curious to know how I had managed to accomplish such a feat without realizing it.

"Now I'm thinking about meaning and purpose all the time; and Spencer," she said, waving a hand toward the dining room and kitchen, "this is *not* it. It's driving me crazy!"

I had to smile at Amy's earnestness and the way she took things so to heart. I loved the way she could take on a challenge or a new idea and dive in all the way, holding nothing back. I remembered her impressive acting skills, the aggressive way she drove a snowmobile, and her spunky way of speaking her mind with no inhibitions whatsoever. I loved the way she approached life with her eyes and mind and heart and the throttle all wide open.

"Well," I pointed out, "it beats living in a concentration camp, right?"

Amy exhaled in frustration, her lips puckering into a slight pout. "How's that supposed to help me?"

"Probably the most famous book ever written on the meaning of life," I explained, "was written by a guy who survived one of the worst concentration camps of World War II. He observed that the people who survived there were able to find meaning in the smallest things, even in the midst of terrible suffering.

"For example, some prisoners, even though they were starving to death, would share their food with their friends. That mattered to them. It made a difference. It had purpose. It lessened the suffering of others, if only minutely. And perceiving that purpose made it meaningful. And even that much meaning gave them a reason to go on living, and those were the sort of people who survived."

Amy's frustration seemed to ease as she considered how serving meals could make a difference.

"A lot of people work just for the paycheck," I pointed out.

"But if I'm relieving hunger and making people happy," she mused, "then that's a lot more meaningful."

"Exactly," I agreed. "Focus on the journey that's always right in front of you instead of some distant destination."

"How come you're so smart?" she asked.

I shrugged my shoulders as if to say, 'Am I?'

"I was kind of hoping you'd advise me to drive straight to Mexico and live on the beach for the rest of my life," she admitted with a smile. "I could make you some good lemonade there, ya know." She winked at me, then stood up and went back to work with the bounce restored to her step.

"Amy told me about your meaning of life idea," Jim said Saturday afternoon as we stopped for lunch after a morning of snowmobiling.

"What did you think?" I asked.

"I like it," he said. "And...I think...if the meaning of Christmas is to give and receive and be grateful, and if that's so satisfying and everybody knows it, then why can't that be the meaning of life all year?"

"Good point," I agreed. "Maybe the Meaning of Christmas is the Meaning of Life. Maybe it's just too hard to keep up the effort unless everyone agrees to participate at the same time."

Jim nodded thoughtfully and took another bite of his sandwich.

37 Love

"I disagree," Amy told me as we set the table for Sunday dinner.

"With what?" I asked, smiling at the abrupt way she blurted out whatever thought happened to cross her mind.

"I don't think that the meaning of Christmas is to give and receive."

"Oh, yeah?" I asked. "Then what?"

"I say it's to love."

I nodded. "Good point. If you give without love, then the gift doesn't have the same effect, does it? On the giver *or* the recipient."

"Yeah," Amy agreed, "but why? I can't figure that out."

"Well," I thought out loud, "a new shirt may be nice...but if someone gives you the shirt because they think you look good in it, then there's a whole new layer of meaning behind the gift."

"So maybe the real gift is love," Amy mused, "and since we can't wrap that up and put it under the tree, we give the shirt."

Later that night as Netta and I sat in the living room and talked, Amy walked in and plopped into a recliner.

"Question," she announced.

"Yes?"

"If love is the meaning of Christmas, then it's probably also the purpose of life, but how can you learn to love?"

"Well," Netta said, "they say if you serve people, then you learn to love them."

"That doesn't make any sense," Amy objected. "I mean, I know it must be true, but I don't understand why."

"Maybe it's because when you serve people, you're not looking for what they can do for you," I pointed out, "and that puts you in an unselfish mode, and that's the only way to experience true love."

"And whenever you take care of something you love," Netta added, "then it matters to you. It becomes yours, in a way, whether it's your child or dog or hometown, and that makes you love it even more."

"So you love things because you love them."

"Precisely," I agreed. "The feeling of love leads to the action of loving, and vice versa."

Amy thought about that and looked satisfied. "Question," she announced again. "How can you tell if you're loving all the way?"

"I guess if you're not losing yourself in service," I said, "then you're not fully loving."

Amy came downstairs in her pajamas later that night and handed me another poem:

"It's really good," I told her, smiling up at her before reading it a second time. "I like it. I'm impressed."

Amy looked pleased, then stood abruptly and left the room.

What are you doing here, anyway?
What do you have to tell the world?
Speak up, boys!
Shout it out loud, girls!
Do not hold yourself
back.

Because what are you doing here, anyway?
What's that thing inside
Scraping
Clawing
Trying
To get out?

Open the cage door wide and
Set it all free
Because that thing
Is you.
It is your very soul.

And what are you doing here, anyway?
Why don't you love
Everyone around you
With your whole incredible,
Beautiful heart?

Why do you keep all
that amazing emotion
Locked up inside
For no one else to see?

Are you afraid?
I don't care.
Are you hurt?
I don't care.
Are you unsure?
I don't care.
Are you vulnerable?
So what?!

Open yourself up,
Let it go
Let it flow
That's why you're here.
That is the *only reason* you are here.

I love you.
I care.
I care too much
And I am afraid.
But here I am!

I love you.
I care.
I'm saying it out loud now.
I am saying this out loud.

I love you.
I care.
I am here.

Courage, Love and the Meaning of Christmas

38 Believe

New Year's Eve arrived and everyone headed to the party at the high school. Balloons and streamers filled the gym and hallways, and a DJ from Evanston played everything from country and Top 40 to Big Band to cater to the diverse crowd ranging from young children to octogenarians.

I danced with Annetta a bit, then we taught my little sisters some western swing. Diane's favorite move was when she stood behind me and let her feet slide forward as I pulled her between my feet and sent her flying to her feet ten feet in front of me.

"My turn!" said Alisha when a polka began.

I looked at her dubiously. "Do you dare?" Alisha looked puzzled, but soon understood as we spun in half-turns around the floor, often tripping over each other and nearly crashing to the floor, which kept us both laughing until we finally gave up altogether.

"My turn," said Amy when a slow song came on. I took her right hand and wrapped my other arm around her waist. She wrapped an arm around my neck and pulled herself close against me.

We shuffled around in a slowly spinning circle. I had to admit that a special bond had grown between us since the rescue. While she rarely expressed her gratitude verbally, I easily sensed it in her subtle actions and in the way she sometimes looked at me.

I let go of her hand when the song ended, and she gave me a tight hug, then smiled shyly and disappeared into the small crowd.

By ten o'clock, I found myself feeling restless. "Let's go for a walk," I told Netta, and we left the gym and strolled hand in hand through the halls.

"Does this seem like New Year's Eve to you?" I asked.

"It's not Time Square, if that's what you mean."

"Yeah. I guess I kinda miss the crowds."

"We could go to Evanston," Netta suggested.

I looked at her with a small grimace. "Would we really find a crowd in a town of twelve thousand people?"

"I don't know," she said. "I hear they have fireworks, at least."

"Let's go," I said, brightening up. I wanted to have fun tonight. I didn't want to begin a new year with boredom. If we stayed here, restlessness was inevitable. A few fireworks might just make the difference. We found our coats and headed outside to my car.

The drive to Evanston would take an hour, but I knew we had made the right decision long before we arrived. Sitting inside my dark, warm car with open fields of wind-blown snow flying by, and bright stars lighting up the black sky, my spirits rose considerably.

I felt the sensation of going somewhere. The motion, the direction, the miles of scenery passing by all felt exciting. We rode out to meet the future head on rather than passively waiting for it to find us.

"Why do you like me?" I asked, feeling invincible, daring to ask questions I'd have been too shy for until recently.

"I can't help it," she replied. She watched me stare out the windshield for a minute and then continued. "You have many admirable traits, for starters. You're determined and bright. You're kind and daring. You like to learn. You're active. I like the way your eyes light up every time we step outside. But mostly…I feel comfortable around you. You make me happy. I just like you.

"Does that answer your question?" she asked when I didn't respond.

"Yes," I told her. "And to think, all this time, I thought you just wanted me for my car."

"And you're beautiful," she added. "Does that bother you?"

"Not when you say it." I had my doubts about whether I was really that good looking, but I wouldn't try to change her mind. *That's what love does,* I thought. *It sees the good.* It doesn't have to ignore the bad, but it focuses on the good and the beautiful.

"I wish I could see myself the way you do," I added.

Annetta thought about that for a moment and asked, "You're not completely on your side, are you?"

"What do you mean?"

"I mean you're not exactly your own best friend."

I had a vague idea what she meant, but glanced at her for clarification anyway.

"A best friend is loyal. He would stand up for you. He would tell everyone about your best side and patiently forgive the insignificant flaws. I think you tend to hold up your flaws to the world as proof that you're not really lovable, and that's simply not true."

"I never thought of it that way," I admitted, "but…."

"But what?"

"I'm not sure I'd feel comfortable going around telling everyone how great I am. Doesn't that seem kind of cocky?"

"It's cocky when you don't believe it deep down inside, and you try to compensate with false bravado. Or when you think you're better than everyone else, but that's not the same thing as liking who you are.

Because when you truly believe in yourself, then you don't need to say anything. You don't need to prove your worth to anyone. You just know it. And you expect everyone else to know it. And because you know it, then everyone else catches on and they believe it, too."

"I guess I could try, but I'm not sure I know how to change such deep-down beliefs."

"Look," she said, sounding a little impatient, "it's not as hard as you're making it seem. You don't have to 'talk yourself into' anything or 'figure it out.' It's not a question of whether or not it's true. Some people just grow up knowing it, and they're no better than everyone else. Everyone else has the same right. You just *decide* to believe it. It's a *choice*.

"Besides," she added, "I'm not sure I can carry on a long-term relationship with someone who doesn't like himself."

"Oh, I can do it," I assured her. "That's easy. I like myself. I *really* like myself. I'm a really great guy, so why wouldn't I?" I was partially joking when I said it, but even so, some of it stuck. It felt good to let myself believe it.

"Oh, yeah?" Annetta asked. "Then say 'I am beautiful.'"

"I am beautiful," I repeated obediently. And again, despite the awkward stretching of my comfort zone, part of me felt good to say so. And I thought that maybe I really could come to fully believe it, and I caught a glimpse of how much happier I would become if I succeeded.

And that, I realized, *is the key to keeping my transformation.* If I didn't have Annetta around to believe in me, I'd have to do it myself.

39 Wishing

We arrived in Evanston in time to walk glove in glove through the crowd, buy cups of steaming hot chocolate, and wander past the holiday lights strung up downtown. We exchanged Happy New Year's with strangers whenever we made eye contact and that led to a brief conversation now and then.

We wandered over to a bridge spanning the Bear River.

"Got any more wishes to make?" I asked, taking off a glove and reaching into my pocket for a pair of coins.

"Of course," Annetta answered, reaching for a coin.

"Only this time," I said, holding the coin over her gloved hand, "you have to make a wish for yourself, okay?"

"For myself, huh?" I set the coin in her gloved hand as she thought over the proposal. She closed her hand around the coin, then opened it again. "A quarter! I can't waste a quarter on a wish for myself!"

"Don't worry," I reassured her. "I have more coins, you can make as many wishes for everybody else as you want."

"It's not that," Annetta said. "I just…I never…I don't want to make a wish for myself."

I thought about that, trying to fathom why she wouldn't wish for herself. "Why not?" I finally asked.

"I don't know," she answered. "Maybe I just don't want to get my hopes up."

"What's wrong with getting your hopes up?"

"Haven't you ever been disappointed?" she asked.

"Plenty," I assured her. "But you can't just give up hoping."

"But why not keep going without getting your hopes up in the first place? Then you keep going and you never get disappointed, either. What's wrong with that?"

I thought for a moment before answering. "Maybe I don't understand what you mean; but for me, hopes and dreams keep me going. They give me something to reach for. What keeps you going if you don't have any hopes or dreams?"

"I just take what comes my way, usually. There are always plenty of options, so it's never a problem." She looked up at the stars and continued. "Moving around so much my whole life, I guess I got used to having to let go of friends and everything I grew familiar with, so eventually I learned to give them up before I ever got attached to them. Is that wrong?"

"I don't know if it's *wrong*, but…," but I still felt that life needs hopes and dreams, that Annetta would be happier if she was willing to make a wish for herself, to get her hopes up just a little. "Well let me ask you this—do you ever get disappointed for other people, when your wishes for them don't turn out?"

"Of course," she answered.

"Then why do you let yourself get your hopes up for them? Why don't you just accept whatever life delivers to them, too?"

"Because I can't help it! How can I not want the best for people who I love? Anyway, most of the time I can do something about it, even if it's just talking to them so they'll know I care."

"I heard somewhere," I said thoughtfully, "that you can't really love other people until you love yourself."

"Are you saying I don't love myself?" Annetta asked. "That's quite the accusation from someone who didn't even know how to like himself half an hour ago."

"No," I answered quickly. "I mean, I don't know. But if loving others means hoping for them, then why wouldn't loving yourself have the same result?"

"Love hopeth all things," she said, quoting Corinthians and nodding thoughtfully. "Maybe you're right. But there's something else."

I instantly recognized the look in her eyes and felt a tiny surge of panic. I hadn't seen it for days, but this was the look she always got right before telling me she didn't want to get serious.

"Every time I wish for something for myself," she explained, "something always goes wrong."

"Like what?" I asked when she didn't continue.

"Like..." she began. "Like everything," she said vaguely.

"I know you're thinking of something specific," I assured her, "so you may as well tell me."

"Like last time I fell in love."

"How long ago was that?" I asked.

"About a year ago. Just before I graduated and moved home." Annetta's eyes looked distant but clear. "Do you really want to hear this?"

"Yeah," I assured her, though I wasn't exactly sure.

"We had been best friends at school and spent a lot of time together. When we started having feelings for each other...things went fast. Within a couple months, we were starting to talk about marriage. One day he calls and says, 'we have to talk.' I could tell something was wrong. It turns out he had run into an old girlfriend, sparks flew, and... that was the end of us," she concluded matter-of-factly.

"I understand that things like that happen," she continued. "What else could he do, considering? But it was still hard to take, and it took months for me to recover, so I decided to be more careful about getting my hopes up in the future. I learned not to let my heart make all the decisions. It doesn't always know what's best for me."

"I see," I said. "So that explains...."

"Yes," Annetta agreed, "that explains why I didn't want to get involved with you."

"And now that you have?"

"I'm not sorry," she answered, turning and wrapping her arms around my waist. "Anyway, you made it impossible to stay away. Being around you melted away all the old hurt and disappointment I didn't know I still carried inside."

"So...it sounds like maybe you're already making wishes for yourself again."

"I guess I am," she agreed. "And you think I should?"

"I can't say 'it couldn't hurt,' because it could; but yeah, I think it's a good idea."

Annetta looked up and watched my eyes for a moment, a light smile on her face. "Okay, I'll give it a try." She put a hand behind my neck and pulled my mouth to hers in a long, gentle kiss. She pulled her body close, burying herself in my thick parka, then stepped back against the edge of the bridge and stared at the shiny coin in her glove.

After thinking for a moment, she closed her eyes and tossed the quarter lightly over her shoulder. The coin made a tinkling sound as it bounced once off the ice, then plopped into the freezing current.

I took a step toward her and wrapped my arms around her again. "How do you feel?" I asked.

"Good," she said. "I think I like this."

"Now then," I said, "tell me your wish."

"I can't do that!" Annetta objected. "Then it won't come true!"

"That's where you're wrong," I said. "That part's a myth. The truth is, if you tell your wish to someone you trust, they can help it come true."

"That makes sense," Annetta conceded, "but...I still don't want to tell. This is all pretty new for me, you know."

"That's all right," I said. "It doesn't matter what you wished for. I'm going to do everything I can to make your dreams come true anyway."

Just then we heard a roar from the crowd several blocks away as they counted down the final seconds of the old year, and colorful fireworks lit up the sky with their brilliant blooms of red, blue, green and gold fire and staccato percussion.

40 New Year

As we approached Amber, I didn't want to take Netta home. I didn't want the night to end. School would begin in just a few days and I could no longer ignore the fast-approaching end of vacation.

When I mentioned this to Netta, she felt the same way. We drove to my house and cuddled on the couch for a while, then I had an idea.

"Let's watch the sunrise," I suggested.

"That won't arrive for several hours," Netta pointed out.

Courage, Love and the Meaning of Christmas

"Let's watch it from the most beautiful place we can find."

We picked up Netta's cross-country skis at her house, then drove back to Grandma's and skied north, away from town, up the snow-packed road, then turned east up a small, tree-filled ravine.

After climbing through the snow for a few minutes, the trees opened into a small clearing about thirty feet across.

"How about this?" I asked. Netta nodded and I went to work. First I gathered dry branches from the edges of the clearing. Then I took off my skis and stomped down a place on the snow to build a fire.

Once the flames began licking the twigs and sticks hungrily, I stomped another hole and lay our skis across it upside down. This made a dry place for Netta and I to sit.

Much of the night passed just staring at the flickering red and yellow flames, Netta leaning against my side with my arms wrapped around her waist. Our eyes sometimes turned upward to stare at the black winter sky.

I felt good. I felt whole. More than ever before, I felt like I belonged. I felt *connected*, and that made all the difference. I no longer needed to seek the meaning of life, because I already had plenty of meaning and satisfaction right here in my arms.

When a bright falling star streaked across the sky, complete with star dust glowing in its wake, I asked Annetta what she wished for.

"I thought you just put those in your pocket," she said.

"You can wish on anything, actually. The key with falling stars is to make your wish while it's still glowing."

By the time the first light appeared over the eastern horizon, the fire had melted a three-foot deep hole in the snow, all the way to the ground. Piles of hot red coals glowed atop a blanket of white ashes. As the black sky turned pale pink, then faded to pale blue, our thoughts turned to the new year, to the future.

"You'll come and visit soon, won't you?"

"To France? That sounds fun. I'll save my pennies."

"And I won't stop hoping you'll come," Annetta promised. "Oops. Did I just give away my wish?"

"Well *now* you did," I laughed. "That's what you get for staying up all night."

"I *am* kind of tired."

We got up and covered the fire with snow, then skied home. Grandma and Mr. Hall were on the phone discussing whether they ought to send out a search party for us as we walked in through the back door.

"Here they are," Grandma said into the telephone handset. "I told you they'd be fine. I'll send Annetta home as soon as I feed her breakfast."

She didn't make it home after breakfast because she fell asleep on the couch while waiting for me to brush my teeth and take her home. I draped a blanket over her and curled up on the floor next to her. School would begin in a few short days, and we both wanted to spend as much time together as possible.

I awoke that afternoon to the sound of Grandma typing away on her new computer. "I have so many email letters from the family that I can scarcely keep up!" she told me excitedly.

Annetta stirred then, and soon I drove her home.

"Hey, Spence," Amy said as we walked into the living room. "Where ya been all night?"

"We built a campfire in the snow."

"Why didn't you build *me* one of those, Nature Boy?" she asked.

"I already had this great snow cave," I answered, "so I thought I might as well use it."

"Ever hear of a chimney? Couldn't you have built one of those in the cave? Would that be too much to ask?"

"Yes."

"I'll let it go this time," Amy said, shaking a finger at me, "because you're such a great guy. But next time, I want a chimney and a warm fire and maybe some popcorn, got it?"

"Come back next year and I'll see what I can arrange."

"Have you ever thanked him?" Annetta asked. "Or do you only tease?"

"Ah, he knows how I really feel," Amy answered. "Don't ya, Spence?"

"I've got an idea," I answered. "That's good enough."

Amy put her arms around me and gave me a tight squeeze.

"I love you, too," I said, looking her in the eye.

Amy beamed up at me, her eyes twinkling, then punched me in the shoulder. "I thought we were gonna keep our little affair a secret," she said.

"It's no use," I said dramatically, "I can't live that way anymore! Please don't ask me to hide my true feelings from the world!"

Amy punched me in the stomach then, harder than I expected, and strode out of the room.

"She likes you," Annetta said. "A lot."

Netta had to work the next afternoon, but the crowds had died down. Drivers passing by on the highway must have been anxious to get home, and very few of them stopped to eat at Becca's. I brought Les Mis and read at a booth when Netta was busy, and talked with her and Jim whenever the diner emptied.

Netta closed the next night as well. I drove home to Grandma's at dark, loaded my things into the car, and said goodbye. Grandma got a couple messages every day now and I didn't worry about her ever feeling apart from her family again.

Leaving the old house was harder than I anticipated. In two weeks, so much of that magical feeling from my childhood had returned, and more. Only knowing that the magic couldn't last forever, that I had to continue on with life, that Netta would also leave soon, and that I couldn't stay happy and content here forever, made it easier to go.

Amy also closed that night. I draped my coat over a bar stool and sat at the bar talking to the sisters, telling stories and laughing. Amy picked up my coat and hung it on the coat rack near the door.

Jim dropped by at closing to say goodbye. "Let's go," he said to Amy after we shook hands for the last time.

Amy walked over to me and stood looking up into my eyes. "Can you read my mind?" she asked.

In her eyes, I read happiness, gratitude, admiration and love. "Yes," I assured her. "And I love you, too."

She threw her arms around my neck and hugged me tight. I wrapped my arms around her and squeezed, lifting her off her feet and spinning around in a slow circle. I could feel her heart beating fast against my chest. As I set her back on the floor, she kissed me on the cheek, then let me go and turned away. I thought I noticed her cheeks had turned bright red as she walked away. "Let's go, Jim," she ordered.

I helped Annetta finish cleaning up and then we sat together in a booth in the dark, with Annetta spun around in the seat and her arms around my neck.

"I remember the first time I saw you," Annetta said, "I watched you through the window when you got out of your car and you looked so handsome. I ran back into the kitchen to make sure I looked all right. Then I thought 'What am I doing? I'll never see this guy again.'

"But then you came in and you had this light in your eyes and you were so confident. And when I found out you were Sophie's grandson and you asked me out, I was so excited, I could hardly wait. I tried to hide it, could you tell?"

"I was too busy trying to impress you," I said. "I just hoped I wouldn't say something dumb and ruin everything."

"I don't know how you could have—I felt like I was talking so much. I hadn't had anyone to talk to about those kinds of ideas for a long time, so it all came spilling out."

"I loved every second of it."

Annetta kissed me. Everything had worked out so well in the end. Almost.

"I thought we were getting used to the idea of moving away from each other," she whispered, "but now that the time's come, I can hardly let you go. It feels like we've left so much unsaid."

After that, we sat in silence for another fifteen minutes. Netta had her arms wrapped around my neck and breathed softly in my ear, each of us lost in our own thoughts and feelings.

"I don't have to be back for class till eight thirty tomorrow morning," I finally said, "but it won't get any easier to leave, will it?"

"The time's gone by so fast," she answered. "Maybe it'll go by fast again until next time we see each other. At least then the waiting will be over, whenever that time comes."

"I'm going to miss you," I said.

"I miss you already," she agreed. "Just get busy with school and all your friends and maybe it won't be so bad."

When I finally took my jacket from the coat hanger at the door, walked out of the diner, and drove west, leaving Amber behind, watching the neon sign of Becca's Diner disappear from my rear-view mirror, I was filled with an intense bittersweet anguish and nearly turned around and went back.

Something felt unfinished and that if I didn't go back, it would stay that way forever. So many plans remained vague and unclear. How could we have failed to discuss the future in greater detail? I knew Annetta loved me, but I didn't know exactly what that meant to her, or what she expected of me.

But I didn't want to ruin the mood tonight by asking such unanswerable questions. We could discuss them later, figure things out as we went along.

And so I ignored the feeling and continued driving west.

Fifteen miles later, the feeling was replaced by a deep inner calm. I drove along with the stereo off, afraid of disturbing the comforting peace. The gentle whistle of the wind as the car plunged through the cold air surrounded me and filled the darkness.

Stopping for gas in Evanston, I stood outside the car and shoved my hands deep into my coat pockets where I found another poem from Amy that she must have slipped into my pocket when she hung up my coat at the cafe. It brought back the exquisite ache of goodbye, but turned it sweet:

You think you know my heart.

But all you know
Is what you see—
A ready smile,
A hug for free,
The outside
Surface part of me.

If you could see inside
Past the easy laugh,
The pranks where I hide,
Then you would know
That when I pause
Beneath the sky,
When I feel
The clouds pass by,
When a tear swells in my eye,
My heart thanks you,
Spencer.

For all you've done.
For all you are:
My dear friend.
My daring rescuer.
My guardian angel.

You save me again and again
Because you are brave and kind
And good,
And so I see new possibilities
In this spinning world
And this dizzy life.

Shaun Roundy

Now I'll never doubt again
Because I have you as my friend.
From the deepest place in my heart,
I love you.

Amy

41 Philosophy

My car emerged from the mouth of Logan Canyon at three a.m. I drove through town to my apartment feeling like a stranger. Nothing had changed here in the few days of my absence, but I had. Everything from the buildings to the shape of the hills felt different, though what I really felt was the contrast between my new self and the old one brought to memory by these familiar sights.

I set my alarm and woke up four hours later for class, but eight o'clock found me standing in the registration line instead of walking toward philosophy class with Ski and Ben. I dropped the class and signed up for French 1010 instead, then walked to Old Main and my new class.

I was surprised to notice that I didn't miss Netta terribly. Instead, a warm feeling of satisfaction filled me and I felt truly happy and optimistic about the future.

I found the classroom a few minutes early and sat near the back. Three minutes later, Julie walked through the door.

"Bonjour!" she said enthusiastically. "I didn't know you were taking French!"

I was surprised to see her, and even more surprised at how happy she seemed to see me. Things must be going well with Ski. "I just added it," I told her.

"What made you decide to add?" she asked with a happy grin, sitting down in the desk next to me.

"Ya never know when you might decide to move to France."

"That sounds so fun!" Julie said, reaching over to touch my hand. "Don't you leave me behind when you go." Her bright blue eyes sparkled as she flashed her perfect smile. I had the distinct impression that her smile meant something more than just a friendly hello. I again felt surprised and confused.

"Did you see Ski much over the break?" I asked.

"Oh, yes. He's so funny!"

"Bonjour, mes étudiantes," the professor said, walking in. "Je m'appelle Madame Frakes. Bienvenu à français mil dix…."

When class ended, I could ask your name in French: "Comment vous appellez-vous?" and answer the same question: "Je m'appelle Spencer."

"When are we going skiing again?" Julie asked as we gathered up our notes and stuffed them and the syllabus into our packs. "I brought my skis up from home."

"How about tomorrow afternoon?" I asked. Getting busy with friends right away, like Annetta suggested, would help me not miss her as much. And I could find out why on earth Julie suddenly seemed so happy to see me.

"Sounds great!" Julie said. "I'll even cook you dinner after." She stood up then and left the room, flashing another happy smile as she walked out the door.

"Looks like you've got it made," said the guy who had sat opposite Julie, the envy showing in his eyes.

"Yeah, I guess," I answered.

I stopped by a computer lab during my hour break between classes and wrote Netta an email. I told her that I got home safely, that I signed up for French, and that I loved and missed her. I thought about mentioning Julie, but decided not to. Julie wasn't an issue. I wasn't interested in her anymore, not now that I had Annetta.

I walked back to the Student Center to wait for my next class. The Sunburst Lounge was full of soft couches and large windows looking out on the snow-covered campus and nearby mountains. I sat down, closed my eyes, and leaned back into the couch as warm sunshine broke through the clouds and shone in through the glass.

"Spencer, buddy, where ya been?" Ski shouted as he plopped down on the couch next to me. "I didn't see ya in class."

"I dropped it," I said. It was good to see him. "And added French."

"No kidding? Well I have some very good news for you."

"What's that?" I asked, already guessing.

"Julie's taking French," he said, bobbing his eyebrows up and down. "And she's anxious to get her hands on you. Now you can study together!"

"Why?"

"What do you mean, why?! So you can get to know her! You know, impress her, take her out, all that."

"I mean why is she so interested in me all of a sudden?"

"Oh, it's not all of a sudden," Ski assured me. "I've been building you up all through the break. She thinks of you as some kind of hero now." Ski laughed like that was the funniest thing he had ever heard. "And she knows you're crazy about her. Don't you let me down, now; don't make me look like a liar."

Ski took a moment to look extremely pleased with himself, then noticed the irony about him being a liar most of the time and laughed out loud again. "Merry Christmas!" he added meaningfully.

I suddenly remembered the last time he had said that as we all separated for Christmas break and finally understood at last what he had meant – what he had planned all along.

"I thought she was only interested in you," I said, wondering how he had managed to change her focus so completely.

"It's like I told you," he explained, "I don't think I could go for the perfect type."

Well, I reasoned to myself, *since Julie's interest in me is all built on lies; it won't last.* I would enjoy her company while I could, and practice seeming confident for as long as I could manage. I observed how my low expectations made it even easier to not feel so nervous about talking with her.

"Why'd you drop philosophy, anyway?" Ski asked.

"I met this girl," I began to answer, "and…."

"Hey, guys!" It was Ben, huffing and puffing. He plopped down on the couch next to Ski. "Man, you walk fast," he said.

"Not fast enough," Ski retorted.

Ben ignored the slam. "Where were you this morning?" Ben asked me. "We saved you a seat."

"*I* saved you a seat," Ski corrected, "and Ben sat in it and saved you the next one."

"I dropped the class," I said.

"Why?" Ben asked, looking surprised and disappointed.

"So he wouldn't have to see you any more than absolutely necessary," Ski answered. "And he met some girl."

"I thought he liked Julie."

"He does. Now shut up and let him talk," Ski commanded. "Now tell us why this girl made you drop the class. I thought you were going to be a philosophy major."

"I changed my mind," I said. "I sort of found the meaning of life."

"Woo! The meaning of life, eh? We'll you're a bit late." Ski opened his backpack and pulled out my philosophy paper. "I picked it up for ya," he said. A large red C+ was scrawled across the top.

"You're not going to be a philosopher?" Ben asked.

"*You're* certainly not going to be a philosopher!" Ski told Ben, pointing an accusing finger and then drawing it back and looking at his fingertip as if it had been contaminated.

"What do you mean?" Ben asked, obviously hurt. "Yes I will...I already...."

"A lover of knowledge?" Ski scoffed. "All you love is to hear yourself talk. That makes you a philo-*self*-er. Not exactly the same thing."

This silenced Ben long enough for Ski to turn back to me. "And you think a girl is the meaning of life? You're beginning to sound like Adam."

"Oh, it's not her," I corrected. "It's something she said. What makes the difference and brings meaning to life is to act with courage and love."

Ski and Ben just looked at each other. "And you bought that?" Ski asked after a pause.

"Listen," I said, "it makes a lot of sense when you think about it."

"Are you sure you've thought about it?" Ski asked. "You think that's better than doing what you want and being great?"

"Yeah," I answered, "I do. And anyway, just doing what you want isn't enough to make you great. Look at Ben, he does what he wants, right? Do you think he's great?"

"Good point," Ski said with relish, enjoying the renewed offended look on Ben's face.

"Don't worry Ben," I said. "We know you have your redeeming qualities."

Ski's smile faded and he looked disappointed in me for making the concession.

"Anyway, Ski," Ben said, "you're not looking very tan. I know you didn't go to Mexico, so don't tell me you always do everything you want."

"A regular Sherlock Holmes we have here," Ski retorted. "But you missed one important clue, inspector. Did I ever say I was great? No, I didn't; so shut up."

"Both of you shut up," I interrupted. "The idea is," I continued, "that if you have courage and love on the inside, then greatness follows on the outside. Get it?"

"Well if that's your argument," Ski pointed out, "then what you're saying is that greatness is the meaning of life, and that courage and love are simply means of attaining it."

"Except that if greatness is the meaning of life, then no one can experience meaning until after they've become great. Love and courage create meaning instantly."

"Hm," Ski said thoughtfully. He smiled broadly and I could tell he found our conversation invigorating and satisfying. It didn't take him long to find his next plan of attack.

"I'm disappointed in you, Spencer," Ski said. "You meet some girl who twists your brain and suddenly you're willing to throw your entire education to one side for one simple, cheesy idea?"

"What?!" I asked, getting drawn deeper into the debate. "You think education's about memorizing facts and ideas? I thought it was about learning to use your own brain."

"Okay, okay," Ski backed off, "but really, didn't you study last semester? Didn't you learn anything of any value to you now?"

"Sometimes academia makes you lose sight of the real things in life," I answered. "We were never meant to base our entire existence on logic alone, you know."

"You haven't answered my question," Ski said. "Are you really going to toss your entire education? Just think about it—there are probably lots of loving, courageous idiots out there. Think of Don Quixote—talk about courage—but did that make him accomplish anything great? No! He just ran around and got in all sorts of trouble and…." Ski ended here, shaking his head.

"Well," Ben started in, "if you'll remember what Sartre said…."

"Ben, will you shut up?!" Ski nearly shouted. "We're trying to have a discussion here!"

"Let him talk," I said. "But Ben, you'd better not be talking just to show off!"

Ben stopped then, looking back and forth at Ski and I. "Never mind," he finally said, speechless for the first time since I met him.

Then came Ski's turn to look back and forth between us. "Was that an example of courage and love?" he asked. "Did you actually silence the philoselfer? Maybe you've got a point after all!"

"I suppose you're right about the education thing," I conceded. "So what would you call it?"

"Wisdom," Ski answered. "Courage, love, and wisdom."

"And that makes it complete?" I asked.

Ski looked down and thought for a moment. "Sure," he answered. "Whatever."

42 Full Circle

It turned out that Julie lived just a few blocks from Ben and me. I picked her up the next afternoon and drove to the mouth of Green Canyon. We parked the car and clicked into our skis, then started up the snow-covered road. We slid forward on one ski, then the other, pushing forward with our poles and gliding up the trail.

"How was your vacation?" I asked. Julie told me about going home to Oregon to see her family for a few days, and about all the fun things she had done with Ski once she returned.

"Why didn't you tell me you're an honorary member of Search and Rescue?" she asked.

So that's what Ski told her, I thought. *I may as well clear this up right now.* "Listen, Julie," I began, "you can't believe everything Ski tells you."

Julie nodded knowingly, almost smugly, yet approvingly. Her expression looked as if she knew something I didn't.

"What's that look for?" I asked.

"Ski told me you'd probably deny everything, and about how modest you are."

I laughed out loud and shook my head, admiring Ski's expertise in weaving his web of lies. Even from miles away, he was winning this game.

When Julie asked about my vacation, I told her about my grandma's house, my family, and Annetta. "We hit it off really well," I said, making it as clear as possible that I wasn't available for another relationship. "I've never met anyone quite like her."

"How long will she be gone?" Julie asked.

"Three years, maybe," I answered. "But I'm planning to visit her in France this summer, and we'll see where it goes from there."

Julie nodded. *There,* I thought, *that should clarify everything.*

Not that I needed to worry about Julie staying interested in me anyway. As soon as she got to know me better, all of Ski's flattering lies would wear thin and she would see me for who I really was.

Until then, I would practice my new confidence on her. I would get to know Julie and perhaps when she lost interest, we could stay friends. Julie seemed smart and fun and interesting, and I certainly wouldn't mind keeping a friend like that.

Three miles later, the trail flattened out and we slid to a stop in a tiny meadow. I recognized the clearing as the spot where I had prayed for answers and miracles during finals week. My prayers had been answered far beyond anything I could have imagined.

Tall pines and leafless white aspen trunks hemmed in the snowy meadow. Bright sunshine poured down through a clear blue sky and made the snow sparkle all around us.

I felt good. I felt present and awake, neither tied to the past nor worried about the future. I felt so *alive*, and a thrill ran all the way down to my toes. *That's the meaning of life, isn't it?* I thought to myself. *To just feel alive.*

"It's *so beautiful*," Julie whispered under her breath.

I turned to her and nodded. "I thought you'd like it."

I glanced up at the sky and noticed a single high, faint cloud. When I was young, I used to lay on the grass after school, staring up at the sky, looking for something above the high clouds, trying to see God up there, trying to sense Him looking down at me. I always pictured Him sort of like my Grandpa, only with a flowing white beard and a sort of patient longing in his expression.

Dear God, I thought to myself. *I know you can hear me. Thanks so much for everything. It's wonderful. In Jesus' name, amen.*

I peered up for a moment longer, watching for some indication that my prayer had reached heaven, then looked down to catch Julie watching my face.

Julie clicked out of her ski bindings and sank five inches deeper into the snow. She stepped toward me and looked up at me with her bright blue eyes sparkling in the sunlight.

A drop of sweat ran down my cheek and stopped on my chin, and Julie reached out a gloved hand and wiped the drop away, one corner of her mouth turning up in a faint smile.

I smiled back at her, then gazed around at the snow-covered mountainsides, tall trees, and bluebird sky. "Isn't life beautiful?" I asked.

"Very," Julie agreed.

The End

of book one

Also enjoy the audiobook version of
The Art of Heart Christmas Trilogy!

bit.ly/christmasaudiobook
bit.ly/christmasaudiobook2
bit.ly/christmasaudiobook3
bit.ly/christmasaudiobook123

**If you enjoyed *Courage, Love and the Meaning of
Christmas*, <u>please</u> say why at bit.ly/artheart1**

Thank You!

Chapters

What Happens Next?

2. The Perfect Gift

Find out in the exciting sequel, *The Perfect Gift*. I'll give you a clue - right from the start, it's not what you expect!

You'll get a good dose of Ski, who is funnier than ever, and other characters. Spencer has a big decision to make, which doesn't turn out quite the way he hoped. That proves to be rather hard on him, but he comes up with a new plan that he feels certain will not fail.

You'll laugh out loud, you'll cry once or twice, and you'll feel like jumping up and cheering!

bit.ly/artheart2

3. The Art of Heart

The trilogy concludes with book three, which is the best book of all! All loose ends are about to get tied up - but not without tying a few new knots to untie first! It's packed with many unpredictable plot twists and surprises, thrilling action and adventure (based on a true story), inspiring character arcs, and dozens of life-changing insights.

For example, lives are again at risk and heroes must step up to save them, romance rolls the plot over and over in surprising yet believable ways, and Spencer discovers, with a little help from Amy, his greatest weakness. Never give up. From the highest of highs to the lowest lows, there is always hope.

bit.ly/artheart3

This. *A Vampire Cure for Forever*

Kayla Porter is an ordinary teenager - or so she thinks, until her nightmares and hopeless crush turn her life down a path of excitement, love, discovery and danger.

Neither "Dracula" nor "Twilight," this unique, award-winning vampire novel shows off Shaun's ability to smoothly intertwine life-changing concepts with unforgettable characters in a highly engaging story. *This.* not only entertains, it will change your perspective of what is possible in your own life if you but open your eyes to see.

Best Female Characters of 2010: Kayla Porter, Honorable Mention
- YA Vampire Books

bit.ly/thisvampire

"Roundy's depth of character development and fast paced action make it a book you can't put down. This is a fabulous book that will open your eyes ... and make you realize "forever" starts with what you enjoy today."
- VampireRomanceBooks.com

"With close to 170 pages and 72 chapters this book is bound to be fast-paced and intense. And it sure is! There's never a dull moment and new twists and turns await with every new chapter."
- YA Vampire Books

75 Search and Rescue Stories

An insider's view of survival, death, and volunteer heroes who tip the balance when things fall apart

88 chapters and 150 photos from Shaun's first 12 years on an active search and rescue team reveal the breathtaking world of volunteer search and rescue. Rescue tales include cliffs, avalanches lakes, rivers, caves and more.

"The best rescue book by far that I've ever read."
- Author Jules Harrel in the Mountain Rescue Association Meridian

Paperback and Kindle: bit.ly/rescuestories
Audiobook: bit.ly/rescueaudio

Courage, Love and the Meaning of Christmas

An American in China
Starting Over

Shaun left in March for a spontaneous six-month voyage through the Orient. Six months later, he didn't return. What did he expect to find by leaving everything behind? His path carries him into the salt spray of dangerously high seas, through frothy, typhoon-swollen rivers, and below shattered, crumbling mountainsides that come crashing down around his feet. Passion for living offered no alternatives.

This journey carries him on motorcycles through crowded city streets and wide-open tropical island beaches, on trains rolling for days across the world's most populous country, starting over again and again and again, discovering what it truly means to live, and what living truly costs. Shaun's engaging writing style will pull you straight into living the adventure. Gather a lifetime of experience in 168 action-packed, heavily illustrated pages. Sometimes it takes a journey of 20,000 miles to finally arrive at one's own heart. Find your ticket to the journey inside An American in China: Starting Over.

Paperback and Kindle: bit.ly/chinaguide

Deep Questions: Know Thyself & The Road of Life

Who asks questions anymore? Smart people, that's who! Interesting people. People worth knowing, and worth keeping around.

The 101 conversation-starter questions inside, plus ~900 follow-up questions, will help you understand yourself more thoroughly, and thereby make the most of your life.

For maximum value, discuss the questions with others to quickly form far deeper and more satisfying connections than you're accustomed to experiencing. You'll wish you made a habit of asking questions, rather than mostly expressing your opinions, years sooner!

UofLIFE.com/books

True You

The Simple Art of Seeing Who You Really Are

Have you ever wondered why eye contact makes people feel uncomfortable? Because it makes you feel exposed, that's why! But why should it make you feel so vulnerable? Are the eyes truly the window to the soul? Can the secret to your true nature be discovered through those tiny stained-glass portals? The definitive answer is: Yes!

The important question is: what will you do about it? Why not dive right in and find out who you really are and who you're meant to become?

Your deep identity has much to offer. It's ready and waiting to show you how to experience your true nature. You'll quickly discover that you are much, much better than anyone told you. You'll develop and experience greater confidence, happiness, satisfaction, purpose, and meaning in life than you ever expected to attain.

bit.ly/trueyoubooks

How to Love Yourself

This Love 301 course from the University of Love not only explains clearly and simply exactly what love is and how it works, it also includes self-love tests to reveal how much room for improvement you have, plus enlightening essays followed by discussion questions, application exercises, commitments to make, and other homework and resources to help you effectively internalize this most valuable of all abilities.

bit.ly/self-love-book

The Motivation Equation

50 Deep Thoughts & Proven Methods for Getting Things Done the Easy Way

The space between getting things done and doing nothing (or doing something else) is usually a lot smaller than you ever imagined. Each story in these 50 chapters illustrates vital aspects of motivation and explains how to easily transform resistant inaction into willing action.

bit.ly/motequation

The Happiness Equation

25 Deep Thoughts & Proven Methods for Catching & Keeping Happiness

The Happiness Equation teaches you many proven methods to increase your happiness easily, deeply, immediately, and permanently. Engaging stories and illustrations introduce concepts and make them memorable, while workshop-style discussion points and action items deepen your grasp. All happiness is not created equal. Three crucial continuums help you measure which kinds are the best and which are worth pursuing.

bit.ly/happyeq

Heal Your Emotions

Practical Guide to Speaking Your Brain's Languages and Turning Pain into Power

This 320-page book walks you through hundreds basic intuitive energy healing techniques that teach you to work *with* your brain rather than against it as most people do.

As your fears and limitations release, you accelerate your progress toward happiness, peace, clarity, abundance, and your true, glorious potential.

bit.ly/healemotions

About the Author

Shaun Roundy earned an MA in English from Utah State University and taught writing there and at Utah Valley University for 15 years. He has published ten books and various articles.

Shaun was born in New Jersey, then moved to Massachussettes, California and Brazil before settling in the Rocky Mountains in Logan, Utah.

He later moved to Spain, Taiwan, China, and Utah Valley, as well as working and traveling in many other states and countries, including a five-week, 2,500 mile ocean voyage to help a friend sail his boat home from Venezuela.

Shaun enjoys spending time in the outdoors, hiking, climbing, mountaineering, camping, skiing, sailing, motorcycling and simply enjoying the fresh air.

He has volunteered on the Utah County Sheriff Search and Rescue team for 23 years, as well as chairing the Mountain Rescue Association's Intermountain Region for 11 years.

He has been interviewed on NPR's *All Things Considered,* and appeared in the Discovery Channel's *Raging Planet - Blizzards* and KUED's award-winning *Secrets of the Lost Canyon* and *Search and Rescue.*

Most of all, Shaun craves beauty, experience, wisdom, connection, fun and adventure, and hopes to share that and make the world a better place.

Photo: Shaun at advanced base camp on a climbing trip to nearly 18,000' in the Chilean Andes with his father in December 2008.

Courage, Love and the Meaning of Christmas

www.ingramcontent.com/pod-product-compliance
Lightning Source LLC
Chambersburg PA
CBHW060831120626
46557CB00001B/458